Naked
on the Inside

by Shirley Ellen Dodding

Enjoy
Shirley Ellen Dodding

DORRANCE
PUBLISHING CO
EST. 1920
PITTSBURGH, PENNSYLVANIA 15238

The contents of this work, including, but not limited to, the accuracy of events, people, and places depicted; opinions expressed; permission to use previously published materials included; and any advice given or actions advocated are solely the responsibility of the author, who assumes all liability for said work and indemnifies the publisher against any claims stemming from publication of the work.

All Rights Reserved
Copyright © 2016 by Shirley Ellen Dodding

No part of this book may be reproduced or transmitted, downloaded, distributed, reverse engineered, or stored in or introduced into any information storage and retrieval system, in any form or by any means, including photocopying and recording, whether electronic or mechanical, now known or hereinafter invented without permission in writing from the publisher.

Dorrance Publishing Co
585 Alpha Drive
Suite 103
Pittsburgh, PA 15238
Visit our website at *www.dorrancebookstore.com*

ISBN: 978-1-4809-3079-7
eISBN: 978-1-4809-3056-8

1

It was the best place to live and the most fun place to grow up. My parents' farm in Alberta, Canada, was on two hundred acres, and it was big to a five-year-old. My friend Stephen said it was bigger than the moon—no, bigger than Superman at the mall. I could not describe it. Everywhere Stephen's dad, Henry, drove us; it looked gigantic. Stephen said there was so much grain, you could never not be standing in grain.

Henry said, "You boys think this is the whole world?"

We said, "Yeah!"

After my porridge, which my mom made me eat every morning, Stephen and I would chase my dog, Ring, out to the barn, and we would frighten all of the chickens. My mom would come out with her long apron on, and we would be in trouble for three days. Other times we would go over to the pigpen and throw rocks in the mud, but never at the pigs. My mom would run out pointing her finger at us, and we would be in trouble for four days. Of course, she thought we were throwing rocks at the pigs. Stephen's dad, Henry, farmed some of our land. I do not know how much, but further than I could count at the time. When Henry was on the tractor, we all went for a ride. The best thing was we could get as dirty as we wanted to and it didn't matter. Of course, when I got home I had to scrub like I was new to soap, and Mom would not let up until I sparkled like a brand-new penny.

    The next day, we did the same thing all over again. Stephen and I ran out to the barn with Ring, bothered the chickens, and bothered the pigs in the pigpen until Mom came out not only with her long white apron on but waving a wooden spoon. On Sundays after mass, we would go to any pond we could find and skim rocks. The shiny flat stones were the smoothest and Ring would try to get the rock before it stopped circling, so we were never great at skimming rocks in ponds. Ring was my beautiful gold and black German Shepherd. I remember one summer my older brother Michael came home from his job at the bank and helped us skim rocks at a lake. After the hot sun went down, we would sit around the campfire and Michael would play his guitar and we would sing songs. Sometimes Michael would sing a funny song, and we would laugh until our marshmallows burned in the cinders and fell off the bald saplings Michael had whittled for us. Our hands were so sticky, we would try to put the sticky part on each other's faces and Mom would get so mad, especially when we were supposed to get ready for bed. Sometimes my bigger brother Samuel would come, and he would help us have some fun. He didn't like flies, and we ran around trying to catch or kill flies for Sam. When we were older, he gave us a nickel a piece if we killed one.

    The stories my brother Michael told us before we went to bed were scary. Every tree shrouded in fog looked like a ghost, and all of the wild turkeys, gophers, woodchucks, and weasels that scurried for cover when Michael made a wolf howl gave Stephen and I endless sleepless nights. The Canada geese, loons, and mallards that floated on the lake gave a cold heartbreaking sound when we were washed up and hiding in our tents under mounds of blankets, complete with the sliver of a flashlight beam.

• • •

Despite the muggy prairie day, all black hats stayed on. No sun poked through the clouds, and no one was smiling. This was the saddest day ever in the lives of the brothers; one of their own was taken. No day would pass from now on to make anything worth smiling about. Michael was the best, but Michael was taken first. Why, why did this senseless accident happen? Why would this be the most important event in the lives of the other two brothers, and why would they be on a path of destruction for the rest of their lives?

Rain fell dark and damp to mock the feelings of the onlookers. Around the coffin, the dirt was piled and growing darker as the clouds exploded into a summer shower. Between his thick black eyelashes, Rick could see his older brother's bed with a lid on it. *Why could he not see him today; it wasn't clear. Was this it, would he never hear Michael sing again, play the guitar, or laugh? Would he never see his mom's face light up when Michael bought her the perfect gift or when he come home from his job at the bank ready to join in the fun? Michael, where are you? I need you now to help me get through this. My body hurts, and I can't cry because this is not real.* His mom was holding his freezing, cold hand tightly. Her hand was also small and felt bereft of all feeling as if there was no blood flowing through it. Mom looked small, Rick thought, like a toy doll standing so still. *Please, Mom, move, talk to me. I need you and I'm scared. I need you to hold me and comfort me and tell me everything will be all right. It will, won't it, it has to, Mom…Mom!*

It was the scraping sound of the shovel that startled him. His nine-year-old jaw moved a fraction just in time to see a pile of dirt flash past his sight and drop, drop like in slow motion onto the lid of his brother's bed. The tiny stones made a pinging sound, but no one else seemed to hear it. No one else was there.

"Come, Rick," his eldest brother Samuel said. "Time to go."

For the next three days, there was no food cooked in the house. Friends and neighbors around brought plates of food and baking, which were placed on the coffee table, by the TV, on the trophy shelf, but all the plastic was still covering them three days later. The door where his mom slept was closed. Rick had not seen her for three days. Nobody told him she was in there, crying, crying, crying until she could not cry anymore.

It was black outside now. It was so quiet. Everyone fell asleep with their clothes on, but Rick could not sleep. He was floating in space, but there was no one to catch him. Where was everyone, where was everyone?

Rick woke up screaming from his nightmare.

"She is taking this hard, but she will be fine. I gave her medicine to calm her nerves. Try to get this sugar water down her at least and give her lots of tea." Dr. Shelton was explicit about his instructions. Auntie Flan listened carefully and gave the medicine, but Rick still did not see his mother, who remained behind the closed bedroom door. Gradually, the front room cleared of sleeping people, and one by one all of the plates covered with plastic disappeared, too.

"Come, eat at the table, little Rick," was Auntie Flan's chirp day after day.

She felt big and smelled clean and was as soft as a bed to hug. Rick liked Auntie Flan. She looked after him, made him eat, made him sleep in his pyjamas and go to bed. She made the night dreams go away, and three weeks later Rick no longer felt like he was floating in space.

"How was school today?" a disembodied voice said to him one day after school.

Rick stole into the kitchen and quietly reached for a cookie off the kitchen counter. It was steaming and he almost dropped it, not because it was hot but he did not know where the voice had come from. "Mom!" He hugged her for the length of time it took for the cookie to cool to being cold and hard. She was back, Rick thought, but so was the time of picking up all his clothes and toys in his room, not spilling at the table, not wearing shoes in the house, and not talking with food in his mouth. Of course, having manners was a large part of the conversation every day.

The days sped by, and so did the cobwebby feeling of what happened to Michael. Nobody talked about him, except for…this was Michael's trophy for baseball, or this was Michael's before he…. There was no word for "death," "dying," or "dead." Jacob, a friend from school, came to play with Rick, and they talked about Miss Hathaway, the teacher: nice, kind, and how she cared about everyone in the whole class.

"I think I'm going to glue a model airplane for the science show. I know I can do a good job." Rick spoke confidently.

"I want to do an experiment with an earthquake or a volcano." Jacob was quick to speak. "Does your mother have any baking soda?" Jacob wanted Rick to scour the kitchen cupboards while his mother was out hanging laundry.

"Of course she has," Rick explained, "but she would notice if any part of it was missing—even a tiny spoonful."

"Oh, yeah, my mother is the same. They act like it's the end of the world if you take one thing."

Jacob knew he needed the baking soda to make his volcano explode for effect. What they did not know was how much everything cost and how little money both of their moms had for things they could not make or grow. Both boys had no father. Rick's dad died by drinking pesticide one night in the woodshed, mistaking it for rum in his state of intoxication. His mom was pregnant with him at the time. Jacob's dad just left one cold January morning chasing a dream and left his mom alone with him and his four brothers.

"I know I can beat you for first prize," Jacob said.

"Yeah, right, you're on." Rick was checking all of the joints in the model airplane he had glued. Rick's mom was preparing dinner, and at that moment she yelled at Rick to get washed up for supper.

"Well, I guess you better go."

Rick turned to Jacob. "See you at school."

Jacob left without a sound.

While a popular piece of music was playing on the stereo, there was a knock at the door. The knock was quiet but still audible, and Rick heard it.

"Mom, someone's at the door!" Rick yelled as he put decals on his airplane, dreaming about his win at the competition.

His mom went to the door. She was tiny in her long flowered dress that flowed out from her belted waist, almost touching her ankles. He was only nine years old—what did he know—but his teacher, Miss Hathaway, dressed the same way. His mom opened the door a crack and froze. Rick was distracted from his airplane. He watched what went on at the door, and he could feel the same feeling he felt at the gravesite all over again. He listened without wanting to.

"Don't worry," his mom was saying. She said the same thing over and over.

There was no dinner that night, and Rick's mom went to lie down in her room once again.

"How was that, Rick, good?" Auntie Flan was so considerate and helped Rick get into his pyjamas after she had arrived and made dinner.

Rick could not sleep that night. He had heard the person at the door.

"I am so sorry. I did not see him. Please forgive me!" Regret and remorse stifled the woman at the door as she stuttered things that Rick did not understand. "I did not see him in the dark, in the rain; he came out of nowhere."

His mom could barely close the door after. She knew this was the lady who had hit Michael. No charges were pending. She was driving the speed limit on a common highway, and Michael crossed the road out of nowhere. He was on foot; he was staggering and he was drunk.

Rick's model airplane won first prize in the school science exhibition. Jacob's volcano would have won second prize if it had not blown up in the classroom. Miss. Hathaway was just about to announce the second-place winner, except he had added a little extra baking soda that he stole from his mom's kitchen, and boom! Rick would remember it later in life as something one would see on New Year's Eve.

• • •

Henry and his wife, Sadie, lived across the street with their children, Stephen and Iris. They helped Rick's mom with all of the chores she could not do, and if they needed to go anywhere Henry and Sadie would take them. They would hitch up the horses, and they would all ride in their old buggy. When it became colder, blankets were needed around everyone's knees, especially if they were going any distance. Henry told the boys the grain was good that year, and as soon as it was all in they would go to a barn dance.

Rick's mom and Auntie Flan and Stephen's mom, Sadie, were baking nonstop. They said if they won the pie-baking contest, they would win a large fat pig for the winter. They were all friends like family, so if one of them won they could be sure the pig would be divided up for all of them to have good bacon and all the other stuff that pigs gave. Rick was told once, but he forgot.

The storms hit really hard that October. Luckily it was later in the month and Henry, with the hired hands, had just brought in the last of the grain when the wind blew the rooftop off the farm instrument shed and sent everyone scurrying for cover. The dance that night was in the big schoolhouse. All of the old people parked their buggies outside, and everyone danced until the sun shone on their faces. Stephen and Jacob and Rick lay like upturned turtles under the benches, fast asleep. The drive home in the early-morning light was the best the boys remembered, and it was amazing to watch the early sunrise stretch and yawn its colors all across the prairie sky. When Rick wrote that in his composition book at school, Miss Hathaway flushed with red as proud as the sunrise.

They had lots of bacon that fall as Auntie Flan, Sadie, and Rick's mom shared first prize. Everyone had great pies, but Rick's mom, being the apron toting mom that she was, won first prize as the best pie baker.

After Michael died, Rick never saw much of his older brother Samuel; he moved to a little town not far away and married a schoolteacher named Evian. In the summer, Rick would visit them. Evian was nice like Auntie Flan, and she would leave him alone to think and figure things out for himself and not bug him. Evian also made great pies, and there was always delicious food.

One October, when Rick turned thirteen, his mom made him a party. They all went to the cabin. It turned out to be an Indian summer after the harvest. They took turns waterskiing, and it was there that Rick's mom looked the happiest. She had always loved the water and hoped that one day she would live close to the ocean and find true happiness. She never did; she continued to live alone until she died many years later from numerous strokes. She was seventy-six.

2

Rick's life took a turn for the better when at twenty he married someone who gave him a new lease on life. She made him forget all of the deaths and sadness in his family. He loved her with a passion he did not know he had. Unknown to him, however, was a constant thought pattern that would not shut down even in his sleep. This voice kept stabbing him mentally. He could not explain it. It came from deep inside him, and he did not know what it was, this dark and lonely feeling. Today it is called many things, chronic depression being the most common. Rick tried to figure out his problems, but it was a burden on any given day; he chose to keep a journal to help him find some answers. With this psychological illness, he turned to another means of getting through each day. He knew drinking was wrong, but….

• • •

In his journal, Rick wrote:

> *I kept busy on purpose, and then when I was not busy my body and mind would not shut down. That's when I turned hard to alcohol, and I knew that it would get rid*

of the demons temporarily, but in the morning the demons were back and I had to start all over again to squelch them. The years went by, but the demons and the drinking got worse. My life was spinning out of control. I worked in my own business, but I was a huge flirt with the women who helped me run my business; I also played baseball and was never home. My wife raised the children almost alone, and my wife, whom I loved dearly, left me four times. She also came back four times. Our lives drifted apart. She had to find her own friends so she could grow as a person. We rarely had friends as couples, and I know when we tried to be friends with others I was again so jealous that it became uncomfortable for her, and we had numerous arguments about my inappropriate behavior at parties. My life, I was sure, would be stopped at the age of forty as my addiction climbed and my desire for help plummeted. I should have asked for help a long time ago, but I was too proud and I thought everyone had these problems. After all, didn't other people drink? As time moved on, my incessant drinking became a problem with any new employer, and I had to move on from some jobs I loved. In yet another self-owned business later on, even the employees (at one time my business financed eleven employees) were beginning to notice the changes in me as I started hiding liquor in my desk at work. I was the boss, so my desk was my domain. At that time, the bills were not getting paid and the banks moved in and took everything. All loans were rescinded, and many business owners in the 1980s lost everything, including their houses. I lost absolutely everything.

• • •

One day years later, when everything was gone, we were just hanging on by renting. My wife was working. I was reading an ad in the local paper; there was a job that interested me and if I had the right aptitude I could apply for it. The aptitude test was next week, but the nerves and the demons were kicking in. Our two children were grown and gone early, and we had a great future ahead of us. My wife achieved a career on her own and continued to work each day. We traveled a little, but nothing seemed to interest me or catch my attention as the demons continued to ravage my brain of all other desire.

When the phone rang, everything else was forgotten. It was Deana, who helped set up games for tournaments in the capital. She was a looker, and of course there was trouble if I looked her way. All of the young girls seemed to be attracted to me, but like one of them said, I was a "narcissist." One day I will look that up and see what it really means.

The long weekend was always a ball weekend—of course, every weekend was, for that matter. My wife was so used to it that she always planned something else to do. We did not have this in common. Come to think of it, when many other couples were gone on holidays I had trouble getting a team together, but I usually found enough players. That, however, gave us no holidays as a family together anywhere, and now that the kids are gone it is too late. The fact that this weekend was a long one and there were more chances to play more games was great. We as a team had won six years in a row on this same weekend, and we were hot! I love ball tournaments; it's probably because I feel my best when I play ball, and unlike a job I can drink all day and nobody cares. At least they may see it but nobody will say anything, especially if I hide a 7Up bottle mixed with white rum in my huge baseball bag. They can't tell. All I know is it keeps the demons at bay and I am relaxed and I can pitch, throw, and catch like a pro.

I put the phone down when Deana hung up. My wife was setting herself up to attend one of her many classes; she was working on a degree, but I was too busy with my team to know about it. There were times when I wish she would come and watch, but then when I look back over the years she had. However, this made it uncomfortable, and if I didn't notice her it appeared as though it didn't matter, so she learned to involve herself in other things.

The newspaper ad was staring at me on the coffee table. I wrote the number down for the test day and left it sitting amongst the numerous other papers that together combined to look like an ill-sewn tablecloth. My mind raced, and I grabbed yet another piece of paper to scribble down the line up for the ballgames. I would leave it sitting amongst the rubble when I left and would have to start all over again later. I had trouble remembering things.

The phone rang, and it was another player. We were to practice that day, and I moved fast to get ready for it.

"Batter up," came the call from our umpire as we practiced until the sun went down. Everyone left to go home to their families, but I would always find someone willing to go out for a drink.

The days were long now that my business was gone. The stress of all the work that it involved was gone, too. I was bored and disinterested in everything, and I needed a challenge to make my days go by more quickly. I took up crosswords with a passion and became so fast at doing them that the day still stretched, yawning in front of me. My wife would have a list of chores that I would do, but I still had a lot of time to spend until I had to start dinner. I reached yet for another piece of paper to scribble something on, and it happened to be the one with the phone number for the aptitude test. I thought, *Oh, well, I'll call and see what it involves. It did say they were looking for someone who was good with numbers and who loved dogs. Well,* I thought, *how perfect is that? I have both of those qualities, and if there was a job with that as a criteria, I had lucked out.*

My whole family had a head for numbers. My brother Samuel could calculate numbers in his head and did so when he singularly drafted up and then constructed a house for one of his sons. My brother Michael had numerous opportunities in the bank and would have extended himself further if he had lived. My dog, Ring Jr., sat in front of me now with those pleading dog eyes and one floppy ear, still wondering when we were going for a walk. I loved dogs, and I was never without a dog. Ring Jr. was beige with black markings. His underbelly was the soft beige of a dried hayfield, and the black markings circled his eyes and stretched down his nose. His black fur and legs were shiny in the sun as he lay there with his large brown eyes full of love for me.

I called the number. My confidence was waning, but after all of those years in sales I could still launch a "sales pitch" and this time it was for me. The lady on the other end of the phone was vivacious and friendly, so I felt comfortable and able to relax. She booked me for an interview time at 3:00 that day and wisely concluded not to dress up too much, which suited me just fine. I shaved and dressed with washed blue jeans and decent sneakers. I looked good with a striped white shirt against my curly dark hair and tanned skin. Yeah, the girls on the ball team were right; I was good looking. I'd look up "narcissism" tomorrow.

I grabbed my car keys and went out to the cool of the garage. I started the engine, revving it to a loud roar, and took off for the address given to me. I circled the area a few times; I was sure I was right. The only thing I saw was a dog shelter, you know, the place where rows of dogs sit in kennels and howl at any sound that goes by. I thought I would go in and check at the office. The sound of dogs whining in the background bothered me a little because I always know that when a dog whines they're lonely. I know lonely—I was born lonely—so I could relate. And there she was, as vivacious as ever, the lady on the phone. She introduced herself as Becky. I knew a female player on my ball team once who was as bubbly as this lady, and surprisingly enough her name was also Becky. My confidence wrapped itself into a warm glow.

"Are you Mr. Csapo?" She offered her hand.

"Yes, but call me Rick."

"Okay, Rick, here are the papers, and you can have a seat over there. Take as long as you need; we're full up today, and these dogs are all looking for something or someone back there. I've got my hands full, and wouldn't you know it, after the long weekend we're always short staffed."

Luckily I had a pencil in my pocket from my constant work on crossword puzzles. She did not offer me one, and my brain buzzed at the prospect that maybe that was the first test, to see how organized one was. Who knows these days? People are goofy about everything. There was no one else in the small room. I was beginning to see why; the whining of the dogs was becoming a howl, and the noise was deafening. I could block it out, however, after years of practice with my mom. Whoops, *Don't go there, Rick,* I had to remind myself. I flipped up the first page; there was one sentence. What the heck was this? I groaned. Great, not another stupid idea of how to trick people into pretending they know something, when all they want to do is write down their name and previous jobs and get out of there. This was a dog kennel, not the Pentagon. The sentence read: "What is the next number in this series of numbers and write how you figured it out." Great, what does this have to do with dogs?! The numbers were 1, 1, 2, 3, 5. I knew these numbers looked familiar; my wife asked me one day to see if I could figure it out for a program she was doing, and I was right. I put in the number and the explanation and left. Big deal if that was what they wanted; no wonder nobody else was in the room. They did not even ask about my previous jobs, could I run a business, nothing. I knew the woman at the front had my phone number, as she had asked for it when I came in. I got into my car and quickly drove off.

No sooner had I parked the car in the garage, the phone was ringing. I grabbed it on the fourth ring before the answering machine kicked in, and Becky was on the other end. She was excited about my answer and response. She said some people had figured it out, but their explanation did not show the depth of intellect I had. I quickly wrote down the address she gave me for the next phase of this so-called "interview process," and I hung up.

The security station was downtown. It was a big red brick building with a training room at the back. I was interviewed by Constable Cliff, a large strapping man, which made my five-foot-eleven slight frame feel like a I was trapped in a teenage body. The back of the station was a training shed for German Shepherds. They were the most beautiful dogs I had ever seen. The fact that I had one at home was noted in conversation, so I guess along with the number question, I was an "in" for the job. All I needed to do was prove that I was liked by the dogs and was able to bring out the best in them. If that was the case, the job was mine. It would pay extremely well, and it was full time. No more boredom at home and trying to fill in each day with some meaningless thing to do. There was one catch; however, that threw my mind into a deep hole: I was not allowed to have the smell of alcohol on my breath around the dogs. Constable Cliff was nice about it, respectful and all, but I was still embarrassed. He said he knew the dogs had sensed it, and this would make it impossible for them to hire me. He said, "You have come with the best qualifications so far. Regardless of what they could smell, they are so comfortable that even our toughest-trained dog is behaving like a puppy." Constable Cliff gave me a month to make a decision. He enlisted me in a program as well, where I had a chance to get sober. I attended, and with all the help and effort of every friend and family member I became a different person. The loneliness stopped, the demons went away, and I was gainfully employed.

3

Freddie was still in the same spot he had held for ten years now, on the side of the street where the shade was the best, and his view was like no other. He was extremely excited today; nobody was there to bother him. Most days the other panhandlers wanted to borrow his blanket or use his personal items, which he now concealed in a metal box, but now there were only a few guys left to worry about.

It was also only three years ago that the majority of these guys were sent off to shelters provided by the city. They made a new bylaw that anyone who wanted to give money to the homeless had to put the money into a black box shaped liked a parking meter downtown. Providing shelters kept the homeless off the streets and also kept them from bothering patrons in the downtown area. All of the storefront owners were happier, and they noticed an increase in their business. *At least the guys are getting clean sheets and showers these days, and good for them*, Freddie thought. *Me, I'm a lone reed. One that bends but does not break. I love the sun on my face in the day and the moon hanging over my head at night. My home is under the bridge on the shores of the quiet waters of the Thompson River. That is my home, but this is my job. My job is here, on the curb of a small but busy town in the interior of British Columbia. At night I exist under the bridge, where I have cover and the basics for a night's rest away from the guys in the shelter. Of course, I have a room there also, as nobody is allowed out anymore with the new bylaw, but I never did like being told what to do. The reason why the cops let me stay under the bridge occasionally is because I work for Rick Csapo. He is a cool guy who really gets me. He and his dog prowl the streets at night to keep everything safe, and his dog knows me well. Everyone should know that dogs don't ask questions or lie or steal or mistrust you just because you might smell or have lost your toothbrush. I love Rick's dog; he and Rick make me feel important. They give me things to look out for, things to watch for, and they have become the reason why I sit here on this curb, sometimes in the shade and sometimes in the sun.*

I look better than I used to; anyone passing me now would not look at me the same way. I stand up when the shops get busy. I know where to go so I am not totally in the same location every hour to draw attention to myself. Today, however, after the long, hot summer, the shade feels good. I see that only a few shopkeepers are out on this Saturday morning. Some of them are out sweeping the front steps or the front sidewalk of their business. The smell of baking from the bakery is always amazing, and if the right person is working I always get the pastries from the day before, even before they are sent off to the guys at the shelter. On cold days, Jennifer will even warm one up for me—or two. She is a tiny little thing but so loving and kind. There are not many like her; she passes no judgment on me, and I need to explain nothing to her. Those kinds of people are rare. She just looks at me with her heart, not a judgmental brain. Jennifer has no family in the city, so maybe we have more in common than we know.

"Hey, Freddie, blueberry today…. Come get a muffin."

I sauntered over, and instead of throwing out the last of the first coffee of the day she offered it to me in a soft cup.

"How are you today? Are you stiff and sore?"

"A little. I have been sitting here for two hours already."

"Come in and get warm. The next rush isn't until 7:00."

"Oh, little missy, what would an old crippled man do without you!"

Freddie sat down on one of the inconspicuous stools in the corner. He watched as the others tidied and swept, and he kept his ears alert for the sharp tongue of the manager, who was nowhere near as hospitable as Jennifer.

"You're looking awful pretty this morning, missy."

"I'm looking for a person coming in today, Freddie. He was very nice to me, and I hope he comes back!"

"Out, out you go!"

From the other side of the counter came the booming voice of the manager as he gave a sideways pointed glance at Jennifer. It was then that she noticed the defeated body of Freddie slinking out the side door. His slightly humped shoulders just missed the corner of the doorframe in his haste to leave. Freddie struck a pose outside as though he hadn't moved from the spot; he was in no hurry to race off at the outrageous mood of the manager, so he kept a look out for Jennifer. She arrived at the door silently, broom in hand, gave her lopsided "I'm sorry" smile, and then took herself quietly back inside. Freddie knew all about how others viewed his lifestyle. The mood and attitude of the public did not surprise him. He knew, however, something they did not know, and that was the real him. Only he knew who he was until his life changed and he was forced out of his own circle of wellbeing and livelihood.

His mind wandered back to that hot summer day when he walked up the aisle of the cement-laced university to accept the degree awarded for excellence in his field. He worked hard day and night to pass every required course it took to obtain a degree in journalism. When his wife and child were murdered, so was Freddie. His insides were torn out, and he was "naked on the inside." His heart beat, but he did not know how. Luckily, if it wasn't for the life-throbbing friendship of his nearest and dearest friend, Phillip, he would not be here today. His days held no meaning. His life on the sidewalk with his panhandler friends felt more like home than any other place he tried to live.

"Hey, Freddie, don't go away!"

Rick was sauntering up the alley with Ring wagging his tail and placing it high on his rump at the sniff of Freddie. The small piece of muffin Freddie had saved was sniffed out of his pocket, and Freddie squirmed and laughed at how smart Ring was. He tried to fool him every time, one time placing it in his shoe, but as usual the well-trained canine knew all of the places within seconds.

"What are you doing still out, Rick? I thought you were home by 7:00 A.M." "Have you seen anything unusual this morning, Fred?" There was a pounding in his heart as he asked the question.

"No, nothing, why? Been running all night?"

"I'm on a case, but I lost the lead. It's starting to baffle me now about the clues I was given, but somehow they led here. If you see anything, let me know. Got to go."

"Yeah, sure, bye, Rick. Hey, Ring, jump!"

As the dog jumped to catch the last of the squished muffin, Freddie heard the ear-piercing sound of a siren! It wasn't long before a runner was speeding by Freddie. He could see Rick and Ring tense and then run quickly as the runner ran into a back alley. They were right on his heels. The man was just as fast, and Freddie watched the trio run.

Jennifer emerged from the bakery. She said, "Who was that?"

Freddie stated what had happened, and Jennifer looked a little dismayed. She saw the man from the back door where she was sweeping up, and she thought he looked familiar.

'That's the man who was in here the other day."

She was so startled, she grabbed Freddie's right elbow and squeezed. Freddie said nothing but placed his opposite hand over her fingers. She smelled good but the cold, empty feeling of how this could easily be his daughter enveloped him so quickly, his knees started to buckle. He had thought before as he meditated on cold nights how

Jennifer and his daughter would be approximately the same age if his daughter had lived. Now he had a deeper feeling for why he stuck around this area of town and continually sauntered back to the bakery.

"He was the guy who was going to come back and see me today!"

"How could this be happening? What did he do?"

Freddie was awestruck. Just as Freddie was about to say something, Rick appeared with the man in his grasp. Ring was panting and had his jaws close to the man's right leg, threatening to take a bite if the man tried to lurch away. The police car stopped right where they were standing, and a police officer jumped out to take the man off Rick's hands. He immediately cuffed him then, ducking his head, placed him into the police car.

Jennifer stared in amazement, and the man stared back. He looked more puzzled than the rest of them. The police officer thanked Rick and patted Ring on the snout. There was no more talk of the man; Jennifer, saddened by this sudden change of events, quietly went back into the bakery. Rick was satisfied that his duty was done and bade Freddie goodbye as he and Ring went home for a huge breakfast.

4

Jennifer was angry. Every time she did well in school, her parents did not even acknowledge her report card, grades, or her existence for that matter. She yearned to have someone, anyone, say she did well or "good for her," but nobody seemed to care or for some reason it did not seem to matter to them. She was born with an inner strength, however, and she knew there was something wrong with the attitude she received from her parents or anyone else in her family. Luckily, there were other people in her life. She was very observant, and she watched other women she knew so she could find out who she wanted to become. She used any motion, gesture, or phrase to help her emulate the women in her life she admired the most. Some of her high school girlfriends would copy the existing cast of a well-received show or movie, but Jennifer wanted to emulate real people, not celebrities. She thought famous people had way too much money and were not real.

It was early in her life, maybe even at the young impressionable age of thirteen, that she discovered her inner strength and observant nature of people, especially of women. This skill gave her an inside quiet knowledge of how women acted and how they projected themselves in a group or in society.

When Jennifer saw the young man she was currently interested in at the bakery getting into the cop car, she fell distraught. Was it not bad enough that she gained no satisfaction from parents or relatives on the home front, but just when it looked as though a handsome, young man looked her way, she had to experience that same emptiness once again? It was as though the only God in the heavens was ignoring her. Did anyone know what she as a young woman needed?

Freddie did. He was a huge homeless man, much like a teddy bear, but when he put his fingers over her hand that day she touched his elbow, she wanted to give him a full-out hug. She felt like he cared, and then when she turned to look at his face for a sliver of a second she was sure he had tears in his eyes. His huge watery blue eyes were right there, right in front of her, but she could not say anything. She did not want to embarrass Freddie.

One day, she promised herself, she would sit down and talk to him and ask him about his life. Did he have a happy childhood? Where did he grow up? Was he ever married, and the most important question she wanted to ask him was, did he have any kids? No worries; there would be time for those types of things. Right now she was perplexed as to the nature of the man taken into the police car. She knew there was something suspicious about him because he looked very surprised, confused, and genuinely hurt when he was cuffed and taken into custody.

Jennifer missed her family. Her brother was a huge lawyer in New York City, but she never saw him. Her parents had split up years ago, but neither one of them obtained a closeness to her over the years. Once when she did happen to have a talk with her brother before he moved away, she learned they were more involved with their rich friends and any schooling had no glory for them. They were both born with money and might be floating on the high seas now, as far as she was concerned. They gave Brandon, her brother, all the money he needed for university and law school, but she would not take any. She wanted to make her own way first. If she needed help in a big way later she would ask, but right now she was too proud. She loved the real people like Freddie and not the plastic people like the ones she grew up with who did not care anymore than her parents if she worked hard or received good grades to better herself.

"Jennifer, I need to talk to you later." Her gregarious manager had a rough voice, but she figured him to be basically harmless.

"My shift ends at three, but I will stay a little longer."

Jennifer gave a smile to the other employees walking through the door who had a later shift. She loved them all. Now, *they* worked hard, she thought. There was no fancy money given to them, and they also looked extremely happy, all of them. She knew that hard work helped them feel good about themselves, and it gave them a great sense of who they were. They were the people she admired. They were the people who would help her become who she wanted to be, someone with fortitude and honor, and yes, in some of their cases a great sense of humor.

She wondered what Gabe, her boss, wanted. She knew she was doing a good job, so she was not worried about termination or anything regarding those matters. *Uh-oh,* she thought, *he is going to talk to me about Freddie, or maybe yell at me about Freddie.*

"The place looks great, Jen!" gloated her fellow employees as they glanced around and proceeded to the back room, where they hung up their outer clothing and put away their lunches. Jen could not help but feel the pride that comes with a job well done. Under her eye on the morning shift, the place was always spotless and all of the products had a little corner of the room that was just for them. The corner for sticky buns, cinnamon buns, and gingerbread men was decorated with streamers and sparkle string that made it look like it came out of a child's wonderland book. Any adult felt like a child the minute their eye caught the dazzling displays Jennifer artistically created, and the sales for the store had quadrupled since Jennifer had taken over the shelving and decorating.

"Look at the cheese corner." Gretchen smiled as she donned her apron for the afternoon shift. "Look at the little mice around the cheese plate."

"They are chocolate dough shaped like little mice with string licorice for their ears and small silver sugar globs for their eyes." Jennifer picked up one to show Gretchen a closer view.

"Oh, they are so cute. I love the way we are able to have a cheese corner now, and the sales skyrocketed as soon as our customers tasted our buns with cheese wedges. That was a great idea you had that day, Jennifer, to showcase the bakery." Gretchen gave her a big hug, and Jennifer was wrapped in a warm glow.

The blue cornflower clock chimed 3:00, and Jen was looking around for Gabe. She quickly straightened the blue irises and white silk flowers in the Dutch vase at the window. Once the tablecloths were oilcloths, but Jennifer asked for a small budget and changed them to crocheted squares, then decorated with blue flowers. The new look was gratifying to the eye, and it seemed as though customers stayed longer for dessert, cheese, and coffee. As each patron left the shop, the aroma of the bakery drifted into the street, and this alone brought in more customers.

Jennifer left the store at 3:15 and had a tear in her eye. Freddie caught sight of her as she was just stepping into her car. He ran over to see what was making her cry, and when she told him he had tears in his eyes also.

"You know that grumpy Gabe who threw you out of the store the other day?"

Freddie just stared at her and was afraid to say anything to interrupt her; he loved it when she would tell him about her day.

Without any judgment in his tone whatsoever, Freddie said, "Yes, I do."

"He just offered me the job of manager!"

Jennifer stared at him through the open window of her car. She looked at his sparse brown hair, blue eyes, and tattered old coat, and could not believe the words she had just said.

"Why is that so hard to believe?"

Freddie was puzzled.

"Why do you look so surprised?"

He was so close to taking her hand in his and sharing the joy with her, but he dare not.

"I have never been so flabbergasted. He went on about how I have created such a warm, inviting environment and how he will support me regarding other ideas I may have to create more business."

It was then that Jennifer looked sad and moved her head down to look at the steering wheel.

"And….?" Freddie was a man of few words.

"And he was very adamant about you not being in the store anymore." Jennifer looked out the passenger window and then really started to cry.

"Oh, little missy, is that all!" He poked around in his tattered coat to find her a handkerchief so she could blow her nose.

"Is it clean?" Jennifer took the plaid handkerchief that was flat but just a little wrinkled, and then she started to laugh and giggle.

"Yes. It's clean." Freddie gave a little sideways grin. "Fresh from the shelter this morning. See? I have no sniffles," and he sniffed just to prove a point to her. "Look, it even smells like Downy."

Freddie pushed it up to her cheeks, and she giggled some more and then she felt sad again.

"I don't want to take the job if you cannot come in, Freddie."

"Now, look here, little missy, you will take the job if I have to tan your hide."

"Yikes, you sound tough." She smiled at him as the sun from the crisp October day cast its beam through her window.

"Yes, I am very tough. There are many ways to get a cup of coffee and a day-old bun," he interjected. "I may even have to buy one." He smiled.

At this he mentioned he had to get moving to get a hot shower before the other guys at the shelter finished their games of chess. He also wanted to let her go so he would not get too involved in her life; it would hurt too much.

"Congratulations, my dear. I am so proud of you."

Jennifer drove home with warm tears cascading down her cheeks. The very words she longed for her parents to say to her many years ago came from a complete stranger.

5

Carlos did not know what happened. He was running, out for a good morning run, nice and early. There he was, the man and his dog, chasing him down an alley. When the policeman grabbed him and cuffed him, he was so humiliated he was dumbstruck. Officer Cliff was nice. He introduced Rick and his canine associate as helping the police on the street. Carlos still listened but did not understand. Oh, sure, he understood English all right but not why he had just been arrested.

"You look very surprised." Officer Cliff was getting an uneasy feeling about the answers he was hearing from Carlos. He had been interrogating him for an hour now, but Carlos kept saying the same thing.

"No, I do not know about any robberies. I am not a robber. Why have you arrested me? I was just out for a morning run."

"You look like the man in this description." Rick was pouring over a paper that described the man: "Five foot eight, dark curly hair, stocky build, and spotted running east downtown. Not to mention that my dog here caught a scent that made him run as fast as you were running. How do you explain that?"

"I cannot be charged for a crime because your dog sniffed me. I have done nothing."

Carlos looked scared. He said he was young, had just arrived from Colombia, and was staying at his sister's here in town. There was a phone number they could call if they wanted to verify his information.

Officer Cliff gave Rick the number that was written down. Rick confirmed that after he had talked to the sister, Carlos was indeed right. He had arrived only two nights ago, and she was taking charge of him until he found a new life in Canada.

Rick and Officer Cliff knew that the robberies happened two weeks ago, and of course Carlos was not even in the country at that time. Within the hour, Carlos was let go and on the street. He was shattered, and he felt like he was slapped. He went home to his sister and she listened to him, gave him a huge meal, and marched down to the Security Station.

After the wrath of the sister, Rick and Officer Cliff both felt as though *they* were slapped. She was young but very forceful about how her brother was treated. They never saw her after that, but Officer Cliff had her phone number and address.

There was something about her attitude that bothered him. It was as though she were the one arrested and they had impinged on her privacy. *That was it,* he thought. *What was she hiding?*

Back to work, Rick and Ring left the building and started their job once again on the street. Ring was given the scent again for the man they were looking for, but it was a dead end now. The chase was off, and no other leads were found that day to fill the description that Rick currently held. He went searching for Freddie.

"Freddie, you need to know the man we arrested was not the man we were looking for. He was all wrong and came into the country two days ago, not two weeks ago."

"Is that so?" Freddie looked at Rick as if to say he could still know something about it. "Maybe he is part of a group, or get this, maybe he came over just to see how the group was doing with all of their robberies. Did you get the who, what, where, why, and how from him? I know there is more; I can feel it." Freddie was in a funny mood, but he was partly serious.

"Freddie, one would think you were a reporter with all of those questions."

Rick leaned down to give Ring an ear rub. Rick did not see how Freddie turned his head and looked the other way. He did not want Rick to know the real truth. He was not ready to talk about his past life and of course what had happened to his wife and daughter. No, there was no way he was going to be forced to spill all that. There was no way....

"Are you okay? Don't worry; we will catch him."

Rick came over and put his hand on Freddie's shoulder. Ring was all over Freddie at this point, and then they both started to laugh.

"I have no muffin today, boy. My little helper at the bakery is doing her new job as a manager, and I have no goodies yet. I will buy one for you next time." He gave Ring some serious rubbing behind both ears and bade himself goodbye.

Freddie quietly slipped along the escarpment and followed the path down to the bridge. There was nobody in sight, and the evening was becoming magical. *This is called twilight,* Freddie thought, *and there is no time of day I prefer better than twilight.*

It seemed as though everyone was gone and he was alone. He managed to scurry down the steep hill to the flat plains under the bridge, and once he spotted his small reserve of personal items and his dry bedding he was able to sit and then relax. He was no dummy. He knew the days ahead were going to be forlorn and sad. He missed Jennifer already, and he knew the black attitude of her boss.

Freddie was no fool regarding why Jennifer was placed in a management position. He had seen this strategy before; her boss wanted to keep her quiet. She saw the man who was arrested and was waiting for him to come back into the bakery that day. Gabe, the owner, saw the sparks between them. *I wonder why it would be a problem.*

These were the thoughts that Freddie had as he lowered his aching body onto his sleeping bag and pulled the heavier covers over his head.

The chill in the air was good for his brain and helped him think, but it was starting to get cold and Freddie knew it was just a matter of time before he had to succumb to the warmth and comfort of the shelter with his homeless friends. He wanted to help Rick and Ring find the man who was in the description first. He knew it was just a matter of time, but during that time he wanted to make sure that Jennifer was also safe.

She was his main worry, his main reason for being there, and the only person who kept his heart beating and his body getting up in the morning. The only one who reminded him of the heartache inflicted on him. The only one who reminded him of his beloved wife and daughter. The only one who made him breathe, and the only one to whom he would give his own life, to make sure she was safe and well. With that, he fell into a deep, deep sleep, and at times his eyelids would flutter and then his eyes would open and he would see the bright stars and illuminating half-moon, and then he would fall back to sleep once again. He would dream that his arm was tightly woven around his wife as they lay in bed, and then he would dream about the sweet, beautiful face of his daughter. He felt "naked on the inside," their loss too great to comprehend.

The phone rang, but he was still asleep. How could a phone ring when he was sleeping under a bridge? He was homeless and did not have a cell phone. The pictures kept playing in his head, over and over. There they were, his wife and daughter. They were getting ready to have lunch in their beautiful home on the river, and they were calling him to join them. Freddie was on his way home from his newspaper job downtown to share lunch with them, but when he arrived the picture that he was seeing now had changed. Everything was different. It was not his beautiful wife and daughter; they were talking and laughing before. His wife was at the stove stirring something, and his eight-year-old daughter was playing on the floor close to the kitchen. They were chatting and laughing, but now the picture showed them lying flat.

Freddie jumped up at the sound of a bird high in the trees. It took him a while to get his sense of balance. At first he did not know where he was, the nightmare was so real. He sat there for a long time. He could not get the images out of his mind....

When Freddie returned home that lunch hour, his life stopped. His heart stopped. Coming through the door, he placed his briefcase on the small table in the front foyer and walked into the kitchen to greet his family.

What he saw there brought him to his knees, and he froze for the time it took him to take in the scene. There was his whole family, his whole life on the floor. The pool of blood was running along the borders of the kitchen floor. He could not look anymore. He could not fathom the whole scene. It took him at least twenty minutes to get up off his knees. He dare not enter the crime scene. He knew from being a decorated journalist that any small detail lost could harbor the entrapment of the killer or killers. Freddie could not cry, he could not scream, he could not yell. It was either his professional training as a journalist or the fact that if he did he would lose "it" forever, and he was afraid of that. Losing himself forever would not help track down and hunt down whomever was responsible for this horrific crime. He crept out on his knees. He had to grab the solid corner wall between the foyer and living room entrance to slowly pull himself up. His mind was blank. He had no feeling in any part of his body. Something told him there was no one else in the room or in the house. It was so quiet. This was not real. *This was not real.*

Freddie took out the cell phone he had at that time, a crucial part of his job and lifestyle then. He dialed 911. The woman on the line could not hear him, but she traced his number for the address and told him she would send out a fleet of vehicles, all of the ones Freddie knew that would come.

When the police arrived and then the ambulance and then the crime scene team, Freddie collapsed. He was taken immediately to the hospital, right downtown, and put on a steady watch.

It took months for all of the details to be dealt with from the scene, the house, the fingerprinting, the murders, and then they were worried about Freddie. All of the response teams knew Freddie. They knew what he was capable of as a professional, and they respected his integrity and intellect for the stories he had covered over his past career. His journalism was poignant but showed great humanity for the victims and their families, as well as looking for a way to help when injustice cruelly plunged a neighborhood.

That was over ten years ago, but Freddie was still not well. He knew that; he knew that he would never be the same. There was no tracing the one lonely half-fingerprint that was found barely discernible on the kitchen counter. The job was professional; Freddie knew that. The crime scene response team knew that, but nobody knew why. Freddie went through every case he had covered from Europe to Asia and back to his hometown in Canada, but nothing fit. There was only one small hope, however, and that was the theft of one item in his house. It was a small mantel clock. The clock was extremely expensive and was passed down from his grandfather from Holland to his father and then to him.

The inside workings of the clock were solid gold. His grandfather was a watchmaker before the war, and this gift to his father and now to him was a treasure. He always knew he should have secured it away, but he wanted to teach his daughter about the war, about his father, his grandfather and the beauty of refined items that were handmade.

Finding the clock may never happen, but he always kept that small piece of hope in his heart. If the clock was found in a pawn shop or in a buyer's home there might be a fingerprint on it still that would match the one on the kitchen counter. Freddie knew that after these many years, that hope was lost. There was no clock found, and there were no further clues to catching the evil man or men who turned his life upside down that day.

He was cold. Standing up on the escarpment, he could see a few people stirring to greet the morning. Oh, what he would give for a hot cup of coffee in a soft cup. His first thought was about Jennifer; would she be there right now? He checked his watch (the one that he found to be the cheapest in the store when he bought it). The homeless were known for being rolled for items that could be sold, so his choices were not expensive—ever.

There she was; he could see her outside sweeping the front of the bakery. It was almost 7:00 A.M.

"Top of the morning to ya, little missy."

"Freddie, oh, have I missed you!" She gave her twisted little smile and touched his forearm.

Freddie felt warm from her touch, and she noticed this. He gave her some money to buy coffee and a muffin. Jennifer took it and rang it in, then she would have a receipt to prove to Gabe, the owner, if there was any trouble. She was not going to be caught by him feeding the homeless and losing her job. She knew she could see Freddie elsewhere.

When Jennifer returned, he asked her how it was going.

"I love it."

"I am so glad. You deserve it!" Freddie stood in the growing morning sunshine and smiled down at her.

"Have you heard any more from the man whom Rick and the officer let go?" Jennifer tried to sweep once more and look nonchalant, but Freddie knew she was still thinking about him.

"No, his name is Carlos, but we have not seen him since."

"Carlos, mmm, it sounds like he is from Latin America."

"He is; he is from Colombia. He is staying with his sister right now, who lives here." "Oh, do you have the address?"

"No, I do not, but Rick does."

"Okay, talk to you soon, Freddie. I am creating a corner from a shipment of Belgian chocolate I have ordered, which will dazzle everyone at Christmas."

"You will dazzle them; I know."

Freddie started to lumber away, his joints still stiff from his campsite under the bridge. Then something started to process in his mind. He turned back.

"Jennifer."

Jennifer turned to see who was calling her and was surprised to see that it was Freddie. *It is the first time he has ever called me by name. It must be very important,* she thought.

"Don't look for the address from anyone. I do not want you trying to locate Carlos and his sister." Freddie was adamant.

"I won't, Freddie!" she yelled back. *How did he know I was thinking of doing that?*

"Because I could tell by your eyes when I told you his name and mentioned that we had his sister's address."

Freddie was in journalism long enough to know people's faces. He knew that look. Jennifer was just putting away the broom and items from her morning work, and in walked Carlos. She was dumbstruck.

"Hi."

His shirt was soaking wet from running, but he had a smile that had her heart strings pulling right across her chest.

"Oh, my goodness, are you all right? I saw how they treated you."

"I am now." His smile became even brighter. "May I purchase a cup of coffee from you?"

Jennifer hustled to the coffee machine and noticed the clock ticking; it was only 7:30 in the morning.

6

Carlos hated being under the thumb of his sister. She was aggressive and bossy, and he felt like a kid in her environment. No wonder her husband had left her; she was a mouthpiece and even though he had only been in the country a short time, he could tell she had no friends and no one to turn to besides himself.

When he heard she went to the Security Station, he was livid. There was no reason for her to overreact. She was like that all the time, and he was embarrassed by her behavior. Yes, he was quite embarrassed himself by the fact that he was arrested, but she did not have to act like a midwife to prove her point. He only knew about her encounter with Rick and Officer Cliff because she came home bragging about it.

Her English was broken, but she was able to indicate what she said to them, and for this his day went from bad to worse. All he could think about was the pretty girl in the bakery. He saw her at the bakery during the morning run when he was arrested. Her image played on his mind; she was young and slim and had light brown hair. She had the most incredible green eyes he had ever seen. In Colombia nobody had green eyes. He was mystified by them and almost haunted; they were so different. It looked as though he would not be able to see her much. All indications were that if he walked into the bakery, they might recognize him as the runner or the man who was arrested. *I know she will*, he thought. *It is so embarrassing. Why is this happening when I had just arrived in the country and have done nothing?* His sister made him eat a big meal again. *Does she want me to get fat*, he thought, *so I don't meet a girl? Maybe she wants me to stay and live with her forever.*

He picked at his dinner. The image of the girl at the bakery was very pronounced in his mind.

"I am going out for a run." Carlos jumped up from the table to distract himself from the food. He was quick so his sister could not pelt him with questions as he ran out the door. Carlos ran for an hour; he was devastated. He ran thinking about nothing except about how unhappy he was in Canada. *Maybe I should go back to Colombia*, he thought. *My mama was gone now and my father was killed, however, I feel totally like a fish out of water here in Canada, whatever that means*, he thought to himself.

There it was, the bakery. He ran up to it and stopped. He was very nervous about going into the store itself. What if she was there? It was close to closing; he could tell by the sign on the window. Maybe she was there. He sauntered into the bakery, which was quite depleted of patrons, and he sat down. The girl who helped him with the menu and took his order was named Gretchen. He could see her name on the nametag.

"Hi," he said. "My name is Carlos. Is the tiny girl with the green eyes here tonight?" "No," Gretchen stated. "She is off at 3:00. Her name is Jennifer."

Carlos acted like it was not a bother and ordered a coffee—very black—then cheese and buns. He was quite hungry after his run plus all of the emotions his sister had drained from him and then the surprise that Jennifer was not there. He was glad that he had learned her name; he did not know her name.

He was able to pay the bill with cash, and then he continued his run. When he arrived home, his sister was in despair. She went on and on about how hard it was to start again in a new country and how it was very expensive. Carlos listened to the best of his ability and then turned in for the night. He was exhausted. There was no escape; his relatives said that even if he went to Canada there would be some prejudice. His aunt and uncle who raised him in Bogota were strict. They brought him up with good values and morals after his parents were gone. His sister, however, was always in trouble. She usually managed to find someone to befriend who was outside of the family realm of respect and hard work.

In Canada they would both have a new start and a better life. After their passports arrived, Carlos and his sister were happy to travel to a new country. They were young, and it was not only the adventure but it was what their aunt and uncle wanted, the chance for them to acquire a better education and to put down roots. This was high on their list.

The unfortunate issue was that his sister, who managed to be in Canada a year before Carlos, found a man too early. He was not what she expected, and when she became overt and hard to control he could not take it anymore. He left.

Carlos wanted to go to school. He knew friends back home who had an education, and he knew friends who did not. The friends who spent time on themselves working on personal growth (as he found out later) were the ones who survived. The ones who had very little education he found out were involved in trafficking and the drug trade and were the ones convicted in robberies. He had to choose. He chose school.

When Carlos identified this as his main purpose, his sister went crazy. She was already struggling with paying the bills, and then she realized the expense of school. Carlos had brought home his ideas for further education and the expense of his courses mapped out for a year. When she phoned her aunt and uncle, they immediately helped out. They filled her bank account, and Carlos was given the gift of money to ensure he had an education.

What Carlos did not understand was where this money came from. His sister told him it was from the family, but Carlos was still in doubt as to whether it was good money or blood money. He knew the structure at home. He knew how hard it was to maintain a steady living. How could his relatives provide for him like this in Canada?

Carlos was besotted with Jennifer. After his classes at the local university, he went to the bakery for buns and cheese, but he really wanted to see her. Now that he knew her shift, he made sure he arrived at lunch or by 3:00. Each time he saw her, he could see that she had qualities he liked. She was kind, thoughtful, and genuinely cared for people.

This was the greatest feeling for Carlos. He had no parents, but he was brought up by relatives. He could sense that there were not a lot of people in her life also. She rarely talked about herself. If he asked her anything, she moved along and tried to sell more buns or cheese. Before he knew it, she was at the next table and the conversation would be stopped.

Carlos wanted to ask her out that day, but just as he was ready to talk to her, in came Rick. Carlos left and did not look sideways; he did not want Rick to recognize him or detain him at all. He went home to his work and school assignments.

7

Rick had chained Ring up outside to one of the bicycle racks. He entered the bakery and spotted Carlos right away. When he looked out the window, he could see Carlos walk by Ring, and sure enough he bent down to pet him and nuzzle his ears. How did Rick know this, he was not sure. However, he had an innate feeling about people, and he was right in this case; Carlos was a good man. Anyone who is kind to animals has a lot of compassion. *That is good*, Rick thought. *At least next time he hopes to catch the right man.*

"Hi, is your name Jennifer?"

What a great way to start. Rick grinned.

Jennifer smiled. She knew this was the detective, but she had not been formally introduced to him. She extended her hand.

"I just wanted to meet you because Freddie has been talking about you a lot."

Rick extended his hand also. He could see she was bright and efficient.

"I just wanted to congratulate you on your new position. You have no idea how Freddie worries and thinks about you on any given day."

"Oh, he is so sweet, just like a teddy bear. Tell him I also think about him. He is back at the shelter now; the days are colder and longer."

Rick knew she was working, and he had to let her go when others came through the front door, so he was quick.

"So, Jennifer, have you ever seen this man before?"

Rick showed a picture of a man who looked very much like Carlos.

Jennifer looked closely for the first time and then was relieved that even though there were similarities, there were also differences. She was happy to exclaim to Rick that she had not seen this man.

Rick left quickly and mentioned that if she did see him to contact his office immediately. He gave her one of his business cards.

Jennifer went back to clearing the tables and sweeping up. She was glad the man was not Carlos. *Boy, it sure looked like him,* she thought. *I sure hope it is not a relative or someone close to him. It is uncanny how they look so similar.*

"Out, out you go!" Gabe was bellowing at someone at the back door.

"Oh, my gosh." Jennifer leaped to the back to see who the poor person was who was receiving all this abuse from her boss. *Please don't let it be Freddie,* she begged.

At the back door, a small dark-haired man was retreating. He was a stranger, and Jennifer had never seen him before. She could see that he was dressed much like Freddie, a tattered coat, pants that were too big for him, and tussled hair.

When Gabe marched down the hallway to his office, Jennifer could still see the man with his back to her walking through the parking lot. She cornered her broom and rushed to him, looking back steadily to see if Gabe was anywhere near the backdoor.

"Hey! Hey!"

She practically slipped on the ice that was forming on the asphalt, and with no coat on she knew she was not going to be out there long.

The man stopped abruptly and turned with a sad look on his face. He knew her only by what Freddie had told him; he knew what she looked like and how Freddie thought of her as his lost daughter.

"Hi, my name is Jennifer. Were you looking for Freddie?"

"Yes, Freddie is a very close friend of mine, and I wanted to see him. I know he is usually on the curb or under the bridge, but I don't see him anywhere. My name is Phillip."

"Freddie is back at the shelter; it is way too cold to be out now. Hi, Phillip, nice to meet you."

Jennifer's teeth were chattering, so Phillip let her go and mentioned to tell Freddie he was looking for him.

When Jennifer ran back inside, Gabe gave her a scowl that could have sent her into next week. If a customer at the till did not look so anxious, Gabe would have let into her. He knew what she was doing. Jennifer took the money at the front, but could not get the man she had just met off her mind. He looked so sweet and humble, she wanted to wrap him up and put him into her closet. She wanted to go out and shop for him and give him new clothing and a haircut. Of course, she felt the same way about Freddie, but she did not do these things. However, she knew she had a big heart for the needy.

When Phillip left the bakery, he was sure he had it right. The boss did not like the homeless, but Jennifer was all heart. He had heard Freddie talk about this many times, but today was the only day that it seemed real to him. *She was sweet,* he thought.

At the shelter, Phillip found Freddie and he had a lot to say about his encounter. There were days when Freddie needed to see Phillip and have someone to talk to, but now that his best friend was right in front of him he could do nothing but stare at him.

"Phillip, it is so great to see you, my friend. I have had numerous days thinking about you." Freddie grabbed his friend and gave him a big hug.

"How are you, Freddie?"

Phillip continued to be one of the most important people in Freddie's life since the murder of his family. Even though this horrific crime was ten years ago, Phillip knew Freddie's heart and all the horror that it held from that first night. Phillip also knew that Jennifer was there for a reason. She had filled his friend's heart with love and comfort, and she was the closest Freddie had come to feeling healed that Phillip could remember.

When Freddie disclosed the latest on crime, Phillip listened with respect. There was a robbery and then someone was caught, and Jennifer knew the man. His name was Carlos, but he was let go. They were still looking for the man who did the robberies.

Phillip lived with his brother on the opposite side of town. His side was a little more respectable, and there was very little crime compared to what his best friend Freddie was used to seeing on his side of the curb. Phillip was thankful for his brother's hospitality but only in the winter months. He himself preferred to be a free spirit, chance it on the streets, and be out in a starry night all summer long.

When Freddie and Phillip were sitting outside the bakery the next day chatting, Jennifer arrived.

"Hey, guys." She sidled up to them and relinquished some jam pastries from her grasp. She knew her boss was gone for the day and was able to give away the day-olds. With coffee in soft cups, Jennifer was able to see their smiles and she felt warm in her heart.

"You are amazing."

Both Phillip and Freddie showered her with praises, and she walked away humbled and satisfied.

The next day Rick arrived, and Jennifer was curious; she wondered what he would want from her this time. No, she did not know the man in his photo, and she feared he would be asking her over and over.

Ring was so beautiful, she could not help but stare at him as Rick was tying him up. His dark coat and tan features were striking, and Jennifer knew that one day she would have a dog similar to that. When she had kids, she would make sure they would grow up with dogs and feel comfortable around them.

Rick was not there on official business. It was early November, and his wife was off to a conference for her career. He stayed behind when she went to the coast. She stayed with her parents during conferences. He was glad for the time alone, but he also missed her. She was exhausted at this break, and it was a good time for her to get away.

The days sped by for him, but it was still hard to know why the man had not shown up in the photo. He began to realize that this man was a "fly by night," as he called persons who were there one day and then vanished into thin air the next. His chase had come to a dead stop, and even Ring could not breathe any life into the case by the scent of an item or a trail. When Rick saw Freddie through the bakery window, he leapt to his feet and ran out. Jennifer was also on high alert. Freddie was ambling up to the front of the store, and she could see he had Phillip with him. They were so close they looked as though they had their arms around each other, but no, it was just how close they were talking. She actually saw Freddie smile, and the warmth in her heart spread like heated coals on an outside fire. She had never seen Freddie smile before. *Phillip was good for him,* she thought.

It had snowed for a week already. Jennifer was excited about Christmas. She had a few more days to wait until her shipment of Belgian chocolates came in, and then she could create an exquisite corner with a beautiful display.

She was glad that Freddie and Phillip were now at the shelter. They had warmth and food and, of course, each other. Then a thought struck her. What if she invited Freddie and Phillip home for Christmas dinner? She would cook and present dinner to them with all the trimmings and then….

Rick was talking to them right now, so she could not ask them directly. It appeared as though Rick was animated and then he left quickly after untying Ring.

"What happened, what's wrong?"

Jennifer could not help but oversee what was causing the air outside to crackle, and when she did ask, she wished she hadn't.

At the same time Rick was chatting with Freddie and Phillip (being introduced to Phillip for the first time), his cell phone rang. Rick answered, then looked and sounded shocked, so he had to flee.

There was no exclaiming what happened, so all three put the alarm out of their minds, and then Jennifer thought to ask her question.

"It is already November, and Christmas is around the corner. Would you guys like to join a single lady, who is learning how to cook, for a grand Christmas dinner?"

They stumbled around the front of the bakery and then sat down on the cement picnic table. They were lost for words.

Finally, Jennifer exclaimed, "Well, what do you guys think? I cannot stand around jawing all day. I have work to do."

"Of course, of course we will." They both spoke in unison and were totally perplexed as to the whole invitation. "But what about your family, Jennifer?"

"Oh, they will not be able to make it this year. My folks live separate lives and are both on the high seas somewhere, and my brother practices law in New York. His wife will have numerous parties for him to attend, as well as one of their own."

Jennifer ran inside, and Phillip said something that Freddie had thought about numerous nights under the bridge.

"She is as lonely as we are."

8

Rick ran to the Security Station. What he received on his cell phone made him sweat. He could not believe that it had happened right under his nose. He found Officer Cliff immediately and was given the details.

"She was found face down on the kitchen floor. Her purse was open on the small kitchen table and the wallet thrown down. She was bleeding so hard, we could not put enough pressure on the aorta and then she was gone."

"Have you found her brother yet?"

"No, but we have all of the officers in the city combing the streets for him, especially where a runner would run."

Rick's cell buzzed on the table, and he snatched it up immediately. "Rick here."

"We found him!" The voice of Officer Karen came through the phone, and she was ecstatic, as she was new on the job.

"Great, where are you?"

"We are just turning around at the truck stop at the Versatile."

"I will meet you here at the station."

Rick immediately set Ring up with food and water. He knew it was going to be a long session.

Carlos was brought in and not looking too happy. He was not cuffed but he might as well be; he looked as though he was arrested for a crime the way he was squirming away from the hold of Officer Cliff.

"What is going on! Again, out for a run." He murmured a long sentence in Spanish and ended with the word "Canada."

Rick felt sorry for him. There was a lot he did not know yet. He was angry, but he would be sad soon.

"Have you been home lately?" was the first question Officer Karen asked. She was new at interrogating but on duty today.

"No, I have been at the university all day, and then I stopped for cheese and buns at the bakery, and then I went for a run."

"We will check the bakery later," replied Karen. "Carlos, please listen carefully. We have something to tell you."

Carlos sat up straight and tall. When he was brought into the station as before, he sat slumped and extremely angry at the alleged accusations. Now he was not so sure. This lady officer looked at him in a strange way. What was she going to tell him?

Officer Karen could tell that he was starting to brace himself for the news. *This is a good indication*, she thought, *that clearly he has no clue about what I am going to say*. Rick and Officer Cliff and Officer Karen sat very still. Neither one of them knew how to break this tragic news to him. They all knew that Officer Karen was to speak to the issue. She started gently by asking Carlos when he saw his sister last. He indicated that she had made him a large breakfast before his first class at the university, which started at 8:30. He had not seen her since due to his classes for the day, his visit to the bakery and then his run.

"Why, is something wrong!" He showed genuine alarm.

"Yes, your sister has been murdered." Officer Karen just said it straight up. She knew there were two ways to state things: just say it point blank or cushion it. She knew Carlos needed the first approach; he was already running out of patience.

Carlos took the news hard. When Carlos slumped in his chair and almost passed out, the officers were concerned. He looked for a garbage can, saw one in the corner, and ran for it. He immediately threw up.

This gave the indication to the officers that he was so stricken that he was promptly ill. Experience told them this was usually not fake. It was quite likely that he did not do the crime. Once Officer Cliff gave him a glass of water and a cloth, he rallied back to a sitting position and was asked questions.

Did he know anyone who may have done this? Did he know the name and whereabouts of her previous husband? Carlos had no answers. He was just stunned. They could not keep him, so he was once again let go and on the street. If there was any time that he wanted to run and run some more, this was it. He ran until his heart beat out of his chest and he was soaking wet.

He stopped at a park downtown that ran parallel with the river and yelled at the sky. "Why! Why!" Was it not bad enough that he had lost his own mother and then his father was killed? He sat on a bench and just cried. He did not want to go home.

The officers said they needed a few days to be at his house and at the crime scene for photographs and fingerprints, so they put him up in a motel. The motel would be close to his house, so he could watch the crime scene workers and police. At least he could run there and watch.

When the time came, he would be back at home. He was not sure as to whether he wanted to be back in the same house where his sister lived and was murdered, but he had no other place to go. He still did not know her bank accounts, and he had no idea how to pay the mortgage or support himself. He was worried about school, although he knew it was paid up for the full year, but he still needed spending money and food. Carlos found the motel, and when he signed in at the front desk the officers had already paid his room for three nights. He found a convenience store, bought himself some groceries, and went into his room to cook a good steak and rest. He was thankful they had paid for a kitchen suite. He slept.

Carlos dreamed he was back in Colombia. He saw his friends playing in his dream when they were all small, and he heard them laughing. His sister was older but didn't play with them. She had her own friends and was very determined to be away from him; he knew he and his friends always bothered her.

The country was beautiful, densely populated, and very busy. Bogota was a huge city with some rich and some poor areas. He could see his uncle and his aunt in their small apartment. There were many times when he wished they could live in a fancier building, much like the ones he saw when he rode his bicycle. So he knew his aunt and uncle were not wealthy. Where did the money come from that they so generously sent him for school?

Numerous times he heard his relatives speaking. They would talk very fast and loud in Spanish. He could hear them talking lovingly, and he could hear them talking angrily in his dream. There was always so much talking.

In his dream, many names were said. He remembered the names now. There were names of his friends and names of adults they spoke about. One conversation they talked about his sister. She had already been in Canada for six months, and the conversation about her was one of worry.

"Why did you let her marry such a man?" His aunt was almost screaming at his uncle.

"I did not know him. What is the problem? She will be fine."

"No, she will not be fine. I feel as though something is very wrong. San Diego will not be good for her."

"That's it, that's his name."

Carlos sat up and immediately blinked at his surroundings. Then he lay down again and remembered where he was. The motel room was semi-dark. How long had he slept?

Carlos grabbed a piece of paper out of the drawer and quickly wrote down the name he had heard in his dream. San Diego…why did that name come to him? Was that the real name of his sister's husband? She never spoke of him. Where would he be now?"

When he was allowed to go back into the house, Carlos promised himself to look for pictures.

He fell back to sleep, feeling very sad about his sister. He still could not believe it.

• • •

Three days later, Carlos was allowed back into his sister's house. He immediately chose not to go into the kitchen but then realized he had to eat. Eating out was expensive, and until he had an interview with her banker he had no money. Meanwhile, he found an address book and phoned his aunt and uncle. They were so devastated at what he had to tell them they could not speak and so they hung up; they promised to call back the next day.

Carlos wanted to ask them to send money, but he just could not after hearing the grief in their voices. When Carlo's aunt and uncle returned the call, they were still very upset. Their next concern was for Carlos. They agree to send him money for food and for spending, and he felt relaxed after that promise. They knew nothing of the mortgage or any finances, so they were happy to hear that Carlos had a meeting with the banker.

There was a will settled by his sister only. Her husband was not on it. Everything she had, she had left to Carlos. He was absolutely numb after the banker read the papers. Carlos had no idea. Then he felt sad because when he lived with her, he wanted to run away from her all the time.

When the banker disclosed that Carlos had ample money for a year, he was determined to change a few things. He also learned that the house was bought outright and there was no mortgage. He was mortgage free at twenty-one.

Months later, with the kitchen repainted and redesigned, he felt as though he was living in a different house. It felt so good, Carlos decided to order a pizza.

When the pizza man arrived, Carlos opened the door and he felt as though he was looking into a mirror. The man looked exactly like him. He just kept looking at him out of the corner of his eye while he counted out the money.

"Busy tonight?" he asked.

"Yes, very busy. We sell good pizza." The man had a Latino accent.

Carlos decided to give him a substantial tip. He was so curious about this man, he asked if they needed any help at the place where he worked.

"No," he said, "we have many employees from the old country. They are so glad to be here, they almost work for nothing. They all want a piece of the Canadian pie."

"So, a person has to be from a far-off country to work for Latino Pizza." Carlos was now very curious.

"Non, non, of course not." He was brisk. "They all like the idea of a place to work to forget the poor where they come from. Many send money back home."

As soon as the man left, Carlos scrambled to the closet. While eating pizza with one hand and rifling through picture boxes with the other, he finally found the box. The box was full of pictures of his sister, standing, walking, or sitting with a man. *This man must be her husband*, he proclaimed in his head. This had to be the one who left her. This had to be San Diego. This had to be San Diego, but he was so old.

When Carlos looked at the picture, the man looked sixty. His sister he knew was only twenty-seven when she came to Canada and was married shortly after that. *Something does not add up*, he thought.

Well, that's easy enough. Carlos ran for the pizza bill and looked at the stamp on top of the receipt. Latino Pizza was located on Colombia Street, so Carlos would check it out. He wished he could have asked his name. Strange that the man did not see their resemblance. Although Carlos gave no indication either that they looked very similar.

After the last delicious piece, the man was right; it was delicious pizza. Carlos downed the rest of his beer and fell asleep. He had to ask his aunt and uncle what age they thought San Diego was when he married his sister.

Over coffee for breakfast, Carlos realized it was time to see Rick. It was time to tell him he found the man in his photo and he was living right here in the city working for a Latino business. It was called Latino Pizza.

9

It was 10:05 in the morning, and Rick was no further in his investigation than he was when Freddie was still sleeping under the bridge on those bright fall days. The man in his picture had disappeared. He kept looking at the photo while rubbing the ears of Ring, lying on the floor beside him.

The door breezed open, and Ring lifted his head up. In walked Carlos, and Rick wanted to hide. He still felt badly that this guy was interrogated about the robberies in the city, accused unjustly, and then his own sister was robbed and murdered.

Of course, Rick was spotted quickly; his desk was right at the front. He chose this position as a ready place for jumping up and running with Ring if he ever needed to leave in a hurry. Of course, this put him at a disadvantage if he was trying to escape the never-ending traffic at the front door of the station.

Carlos wasted no time in telling him that he was sure the man in the photo Rick had was the same man who delivered a pizza the night before. Rick could feel his heart beating faster, and of course Ring was alert as well. Ring was so alert that both of his ears were pointed straight up and he was trotting back and forth in front of Rick's desk.

"Sit, Ring, sit," was the command given.

Overwhelmed with this new information, Rick thanked Carlos and leashed up his dog. Colombia Street was not far from the station, and he knew the run would do him good. On Colombia Street, Rick Csapo and his dog, Ring, looked up and down for Latino Pizza. There was no such place. Rick sat on a short brick wall and thought about it. Some of the houses on this street were the older homes of the city. Why would they have a stamped receipt and be able to deliver an actual pizza if there was no such place? Then he saw the van; it had a metallic sign that said "Latino Pizza, delivered hot." So it was delivered out of the back of a small warehouse. Rick knew what this meant. It meant all kinds of things.

Now that he knew the location, Rick lurched Ring forward and ran back to the station to inform Officer Cliff of his find. Officer Cliff was tied up on the phone, and when he hung up he grabbed his blazer and ran out the door. Rick and Ring were both panting from the run back.

"Rick, you look just like your dog." He grinned as he jerked past them.

"I need to talk to you!" Rick yelled at him as he was striding his way down the hallway to the back door.

"Gotta go, talk later."

"Okay. I'll be at City Hall." Rick knew he wanted to check on the date the pizza business started up. He knew all of the records would be there. *It could not have been too long ago,* he thought. *Never heard of Latino Pizza.*

When Rick found the counter at City Hall for business licenses, he asked the clerk to check on the date that Latino Pizza started up. Of course he had to give his badge to show who he was, although most of the officials in the city knew him. He also needed clearance for his dog to enter the building. He could have left him outside, but Rick was a little excited about the latest event and he knew Ring was also. Ring needed reassurance of calm, just enough to have his pointed ears relax.

The clerk had no record of Latino Pizza. She indicated she would need to look at another file of the most recent businesses in the last month. Sure enough, Latino Pizza had opened up only three weeks ago. *Well, isn't that interesting*, Rick thought. *What are they hiding back there, and what are they covering up? Carlos phoned them, and they delivered. Who says they are hiding anything, just because they are hidden and situated behind a busy street? It is just odd that he had not noticed them or heard of them before, when he is downtown all the time.* Rick sat outside City Hall on the circular cement bench with Ring, ears like radar. Then he had an idea.

Tying Ring up to the bicycle rack, he quickly went back inside. When he spotted the same clerk behind the counter, he asked her, "If a business owner wants to buy a metallic sign for a van or vehicle to advertise their business, where would they purchase such a thing?" Rick knew the answer just as he was asking it.

"Look in the phone book under 'signs.'"

The clerk mentioned that even if he was wanting to know the date the new business bought a sign, the sign company would not release that information.

"Not even to a detective." Rick was perplexed as he rifled through the telephone book. He wrote down three addresses and after scratching both of Ring's ears, he untied him and they were now on a hunt for new information.

All of the sign companies were up near the Industrial Park. Rick knew this was higher up on the hills, and with the newly fallen snow he would have to wait until conditions allowed it. Meanwhile, he would see Freddie and maybe have a warm hot chocolate with him and Phillip if they were around.

The bakery was thriving. Every table inside was taken, and Jennifer was flushed with energy. Whenever the store was full and there was a line up at the counter, she could not help but feel ecstatic at how the business was thriving. Maybe for the winter she would start to sell a thick soup that she knew her grandmother loved and that her mother taught her servants how to make. She could barely remember servants.

Rick found Freddie and Phillip sitting at a corner table inside. They looked fit and healthy and very cleaned up, Rick thought. They were allowed in now because they were cleaned up and they paid.

On their little round table were scones and hot chocolate, and they motioned for Rick to join them. When he did, he noticed that the traditional Dutch blue tablecloths and flower vases were gone and they were transplanted with Christmas colors and Christmas décor.

Jennifer had outdone herself again. When she arrived Rick commented on her excellent taste, and he thought he saw a blush creep into her cheeks. Where he was sitting, he looked up and saw the corner where she had made a display of Belgian chocolate. He was not a chocolate lover, but he could be after seeing this display. It had fake snow and crystals set into the wall. Snowflakes hung down on string, and little skiers were seen in the fabric that was a spongy white. At the small chalet, every wall on each of the boutiques in the village was a chocolate slab. There was a wrap on each one advertising the chocolates of Belgium. The sales in the bakery reached a new height. The chocolate that was also served as hot chocolate was the finest chocolate from Belgium.

"This is no longer a bakery. This is a European café."

The lady next to Rick was spouting this excitement as her plump arm hoisted up yet another hot cup of chocolate and a large dark piece of chocolate filled with nuts.

10

After a few buns, cheese, and hot chocolate, Rick informed Freddie of the new lead found at Latino Pizza. Phillip had gone to the restroom, and Rick could not wait to indulge Freddie with his new information. Freddie was ecstatic to be in on the case, and he vowed he would be his homeless self and sift through the garbage on Colombia Street, finding a way to be in the face of the guys who deliver pizza.

Rick did not want him snooping, being caught or questioned, so Freddie indicated he would just be a street guy and maybe ask for some leftover crusts. Rick was not sure of this approach, especially if they ever saw Rick and Freddie talking together; they might figure out that he was a snitch. When Phillip arrived back at the table and Jennifer indicated her shift was about to end, all three left.

Rick untied Ring from the outside bicycle rack and headed away from the bakery. Ring was not sure about going; he had found a warm spot with a solitary sunbeam on the snow and was happy for the rest.

"Come on, boy, we have work to do."

Ring was up at the command of Rick's voice, and the two of them were off. Downtown on Colombia Street, the snow was still coming down so hard that Rick decided to call it a day. They would wait for the next dry day to climb the hills to locate a sign company that sold the Latino Pizza business a metallic sign. Meanwhile, Rick wanted to see how Freddie was looking at slinking around the place. Freddie indicated he would be on it immediately.

Rick and Ring walked to the location on Colombia Street. When Rick arrived at the location, the snow was so heavy he could not see Freddie. Then he saw what he had come to see. The van was there and Freddie was also there, moving garbage cans right in front of the house. "Oh, my gosh." Rick was astounded. He tried to keep Ring quiet. He recognized Freddie and was starting to get excited.

As soon as Freddie could hear movement behind him, he looked through the mess in front of him and threw Ring a pork chop bone. He knew Rick would be worried that Ring would bark. As soon as they gave their secret wave to each other, Rick moved on and ran out of the area after Ring had enjoyed his treat.

Rick knew Freddie would be all right and he would move quickly so as not to be found out or lingering.

Rick and Ring headed home for a rest.

• • •

Carlos was frantic about San Diego. He was sure his sister married a young man, not the father figure he saw in the picture. He had no choice but to sift through all of the other pictures and maybe find something else that would suit his imagination. He imagined a strong, dark young man closer to the age of his sister. Why else would she have married him in such a short time? What was the draw if he was old and white haired? He had no idea. Somehow he had a desire to know. His aunt and uncle knew his name, but he wondered if they knew what he looked like. They had never arrived in Canada to meet him, and assuredly his sister had not sent them pictures.

I wonder if she was afraid of him or what he represented. There must be a way to find out about this man.

If he took the pictures around town or even offered them to the police, maybe he could find out more. Also, the police wanted to know more. Maybe they could trace something about him. He would ask Rick for help; he liked Rick. He could tell Rick felt badly about how he was treated by the police; it was just a feeling he got.

Before he left to seek out Rick, Carlos decided to phone his aunt and uncle in Bogota. There was no burial for his sister, and now that it had been four months Carlos thought his aunt and uncle would be a little calmer about everything. Somehow Carlos thought maybe they blamed him for something. He was never to find out. His aunt and uncle did not answer the phone, and when he phoned numerous times throughout the day he finally checked out the number. The number was cancelled and no longer available. He had no way to find out where his relatives went and no phone number to tie him to them. He wondered why.

With the fast-falling snow, Carlos decided to take the bus downtown. As he entered the station, Carlos saw that Rick and Ring were nowhere to be found. They had left for the day, so Carlos chose to walk to the bakery. He knew it would be a hike in the snow, but he was prepared for it. He always had a backpack and carried a woolen sweater and a rain jacket. He carried a hat that he had always worn in Colombia. It was knitted, one that his aunt had made, and thinking about that had made him very sad. He could not figure out where they could have gone. He was still interested in Jennifer, but his thoughts kept going back to his relatives. He had an uneasy feeling about it. Why was his sister's wallet thrown down? Why was she robbed and then murdered? Why had his relatives in Colombia disappeared all of a sudden shortly after her death?

Carlos kept walking steadily in the falling snow. It was difficult to see in front of him, the snow was so thick. On the side of the road there were stalled cars, and amidst the rows of cars there were snow piles blended with darker areas, which were stones, rocks, and salt.

He never saw this in South America; there was snow but in the higher peaks.

When Carlos arrived at the bakery, it was after three and Jennifer had left. He felt sad all over again. It was just then that he saw Gretchen, and she acknowledged him with a smile. "Hey, Carlos, how's it going? How is school?"

"We are off for Christmas break now. My last exam was yesterday."

"So, what are you doing for Christmas?"

Gretchen looked at him and was sorry she asked. He seemed preoccupied. Carlos did not answer at first. He was deep in thought. The fact that Jennifer was not there when he needed her put him into a different head space.

"Are you all right?" Gretchen asked him nicely and not intrusively.

"Oh, just a little preoccupied about my sister and my relatives." He wanted to confess to someone about everything, but that special someone was not there. Maybe her colleague and friend by the name of Gretchen would be an appropriate substitute.

"Jennifer will not be in until after the holiday weekend."

"Where is she going?" Carlos was frantic that he would not see her.

"She is not going anywhere, but she is having company for Christmas dinner." Gretchen was on her way to set up another table.

"Oh, I thought she had no family in town." Carlos looked and sounded disappointed.

"No, she has no family in town. She is just inviting friends over to practice her cooking skills." Gretchen grinned at this but kept working.

"Oh." Carlos paid his money and left.

Walking down the hill, Carlos never felt so alone. He had no sister, no aunt and uncle, and nobody in town to go home to. Usually he did not feel sorry for himself, but today he did.

11

Jennifer walked into her condo and threw her grocery bags onto the table. Outside the snow was drifting onto all the window ledges, her outside chair, and her swinging nameplate. Her name, Jennifer Shields, was almost covered. She wished her mom and dad and brother were around. She needed someone to talk to, to share her life with, and to snuggle up to, especially on a cold wintry day like today.

On the phone table lay two postcards: one from her mom and one from her dad. They were both with different people in hot parts of the world. Her mom was in the Azures, and her dad was in Barcelona. They sounded happy and relaxed, but she still wished for a home and home life that was not broken or fractured in any way. *The people who have a solid family life are so lucky,* she thought, and then she sat down. She thought of Freddie and Phillip. She knew Phillip had a brother in town, but she knew he had no wife or children. Poor Freddie. One day she promised herself she would get him to talk about his past. He was closed but still wonderful in his own way.

On her way over to the Christmas tree, Jennifer picked up her cat, Sparky, and stroked his fur. She loved his smooth fur, and she snuggled her nose into his soft neck. The stress she felt about not seeing her parents this Christmas and not having family around melted like chocolate on a hot day. Her thoughts went to the store and her love of decorating and, of course, her chocolate corner. When she realized it was already the 23rd of December, she knew she would be making a turkey dinner in a couple of days, so she had to get to work. She put away the groceries and took a shower. She would be making a full Christmas dinner, and she would have two guests over. She was a little nervous about this. She turned eighteen in the new year, but she was confident she could pull this off. She had never made a huge dinner before with all of the trimmings. She would have to rely on her memory when she sat as a little girl on a stool and watched the head cook of her parents' house create a masterpiece.

Maybe, with a warm dinner and a little drink, I could get Freddie talking. He would feel comfortable with his best friend Phillip beside him and yes, just maybe he would reveal his inner self.

It was great, she thought, to not be working these next two days. The shop would be closed early on Christmas Eve anyway, so she was not feeling too guilty. *I wonder if Carlos had stopped by.* She could phone Gretchen to check, but Gretchen had her own life.

He was the other person she wondered about. Was Carlos going to be all right this Christmas? What was he going to be doing with his sister gone? Does he have a place to go for the holiday meal?

It was at that moment Jennifer realized she had left her extra ingredients at the shop. She had shopped for what she needed on her lunch breaks at the large shopping center. Under her breath, she was mad at herself for forgetting the bag of sage and sausage, especially for the stuffing. It was in the fridge at the bakery. Looking outside, she knew she could not drive. Luckily she had bought her condo close to her work, so she ventured out to walk the short distance. Grabbing a wool hat and scarf and donning her thickest jacket, she ducked her head down from the falling snow outside and plunged forward. She had both keys to the store and to her condo, so she was set. The wind whipped itself around her body and she breathed deeply, enough to know that it was not a good idea. The next time she breathed with her scarf over her mouth.

She practically slid down the small hill to the outside cropping of small businesses, where the bakery was located. It was then she saw the form of a man walking away from the store. He was sporting a knitted hat and a scarf and carrying a backpack.

Oh my gosh; that has to be Carlos, she breathed.

"Carlos, Carlos!" She practically screamed his name into the wind.

Just then a car swooshed by and splashed her with mud and hard snow. She hesitated and then slipped. Carlos came running to grab her, and then it was magic. He looked at her and then looked away. She looked at him and then started brushing off the snow. He helped her in an awkward way ,and eventually when she was righted she was standing square in front of him. He looked down at her sparkling green eyes, and she felt the same warmth inside as she did the first time she saw him, like hot coals on a summer day.

He could not resist her green eyes; he kept staring and all of a sudden she planted a whisper of a kiss on his lips.

Carlos went very stiff; he was not used to a woman making the first move. Once he realized it did not matter, he started to relax and then he kissed her back with all the passion he had felt for months.

Jennifer was stunned as to the intensity of his kiss and a little blown off center. She moved both of them off the curb of the busy street and let go of his arms. They looked into each other's eyes, and then they both started to laugh.

"Where were you going just now?" Jennifer was curious to see if he went to the bakery looking for her.

"I was just leaving to go home. I had a bun and cheese and talked to Gretchen. She said you were gone for the holiday and then, well, yes, I felt very sad, as I did not know how to contact you. But I am glad you are here now."

"Me too." Jennifer could not say any more. She was so entranced.

"Let's go somewhere for a coffee. The bakery is closed now."

"How about if you follow me to the bakery just for a moment? I have the keys, and I need to collect some items from the back fridge."

Carlos was so happy to see her that he would go anywhere with her, and so they trudged around the snowbanks and stopped at the door. Just then they saw one of the bakery trucks spin its tires and find its way to the main street.

"That's odd. I thought Gabe was already gone for the holidays." Jennifer turned to Carlos and looked puzzled.

She turned the key and found her way to the back room. Opening the fridge, she could see that Gretchen had done a good job of clearing away all of the items not needed for the three days they were closed, but her bag was still there. She checked and inside were the items she had bought for her dinner, plus some small milk containers given to her that would not be used at the bakery over the holiday.

All the time she was searching, her mind was racing. She wanted to invite Carlos to her house for a drink or hot chocolate but felt a little nervous about it. Oh, well, all she had to do was ask him.

On the way out the door and after locking up the bakery, Jennifer asked. Carlos was ready with a quick yes, and they both walked back the other way to her condo.

He was quiet but listened to her story about how she found the condo shortly after she moved to the city. Her parents were physically not in her life, but their money was and they purchased the condo outright for her. She realized later that it may not be a good thing to tell. Who knows how people react to being with someone who need not struggle with finances? When Carlos confessed about his unique situation, she felt almost relieved. He stated that his sister left everything to him and that he was mortgage free at twenty-one.

When Jennifer and Carlos settled with a hot Christmas drink, she felt very comfortable and realized they had a lot in common.

He had no family in the city, and neither did she. He had no siblings (his sister's recent murder looming in his mind), and she had one brother in New York. At least he had an aunt and uncle he could rely on.

After Carlos told Jennifer about the strange disappearance of his aunt and uncle, she rose from the couch and fumbled around in the kitchen. She looked back at Carlos and thought, *He is as lonely as I am.*

"Let's order some pizza!" She was adamant about changing the subject.

Carlos was staring at the tree with her cat, Sparky, curled up in his lap. He did not hear her at first.

12

It was Friday afternoon, just before Jennifer went home. The time was 3:00 P.M., and Gretchen knew Jennifer was sad.

"Jen, please tell me what's wrong." Gretchen's previous pleading had not been heard. "I need a change. I am constantly serving and creating." Her slow body language showed no energy; she was dragging herself through every shift.

"I know what you need; you need to get out of town. Let's go shopping for the day or even spend the night; let's go to Vernon." Gretchen knew there was a great shop there, and it was an hour away.

Jennifer kept thinking about that day. She loved Gretchen, but driving through the snow on that day made Jennifer nervous. By the time they arrived, the streets were full of snow and it was difficult to claim a parking spot.

Gretchen circled the area twice and then sidled up to an ancient truck. The driver was walking past the fender and had his keys in his hands.

"He looks like he came from a ranch. What a cutie. Look at those tight jeans and cowboy hat. Hey, do you need your spot?"

"Nope, just leaving, ladies." He tipped his hat and gave a Clint Eastwood smile. "Mmm, he could put his boots under my bed." Gretchen was all grin.

"Yikes, who am I with?" Jennifer could not help but grin herself.

"We need more of that stuff!" Gretchen squealed as she turned her wheel into place and the car jolted against the curb.

"Where are we going?" Jennifer peaked through the frosty car window and was all anticipation.

"It is the best antique shop in the interior. You will love it."

The area in front of the door was icy, and they half slid into it. Jennifer could not believe her eyes. The door itself was gigantic; she remembered standing back to admire the carving and the details in the wood panel. The artist had carved trees and climbing bears all around the edges. That she would never forget.

As she snuggled her cat, Sparky, and checked her tree lights, Jennifer remembered the store; it was huge and every corner and every item was talking to her. "Please buy me." It was a strange feeling, but it was how she felt on that particular day. *Why is this feeling so strong? What is in here that is tempting my pocketbook?* Jennifer felt haunted.

In her mind, Jennifer could see the images well. Gretchen kept putting her hands on all of the wood bureaus, and there were many. Some were long and wide and fashioned out of dark mahogany, and some were tall and elegant and made out of Belgian oak. She was besotted with the incredible china displayed on all of the furniture. The man who owned the store was either good at setting up displays or he had a gifted employee to help him. Sparky was restless. She put him down on the floor, and he proceeded to bat the tree decorations like they were soccer balls. Jennifer moved the Christmas bulbs up higher, then Sparky went after the tinsel. She remembered reading about tinsel and pets and that it was a choking hazard, so Jennifer moved all of the tinsel up higher. She must have been daydreaming when she decorated the tree. Why had she not done that before?

Jennifer realized she was one day away from her Christmas dinner, and she was feeling the stress. *Of course, yesterday with Carlos did not help*, she thought. What a dream guy. She could not get the feel of his kiss off her lips. She invited him for dinner. She could not believe she actually did; she invited him to dinner! Now there would be Freddie, Phillip, herself, and now Carlos. Why on earth had she done that?

Now dreading her sudden and impulsive move, she was waiting for his phone call to confirm. It could be a stall tactic; he was extremely shy. *Oh, well.* Walking around the house, she checked the tables and mantel for dust. She was extremely proud of her fireplace, beautiful in chalk white with pastel flowers painted down the sides. Her flower vases were full, and then she ran her hand over the mantel clock in the middle of the flower arrangement.

Now that was the item that was calling her name in the antique store! No sooner had she looked behind the tall Belgian oak bureau, there it was, standing elegantly next to a beautifully displayed array of Royal Albert China reflected in a back wall mirror. What a beauty. The round top gave it grace. It stood eight inches tall and fourteen inches long, with a top that curved like a French Foreign Legion hat. It was golden like the sun peeking through a straw hat in summer, wispy and fairylike. The clock hands were so bright, they reflected the late-afternoon sunbeam that shot through the room. There was something about the mantel clock that was magical, but she could not figure out what it was. She dreamed it came from a glorious place, and now it had found its way into her home and heart.

Jennifer remembered bartering for it. The man was not impressed.

"This is not Mexico." He was quick to correct.

"I know, but I do want it, and of course your price is too high for a working girl. I am not a collector, and I am not out to steal it."

"Well, then, what do you call it? It is priced at $500.00, and you want to offer only $250.00." He was grim and adamant.

"You know, I live in another city and I will take my money back to the stores there, even if I have to buy a new one at a jewelry store." Jennifer dug in and would not relent.

"How many sales have you had today in this snow? I do not see many people in the store."

Gretchen was becoming embarrassed. "Jen," she said. "You're tired; let's go."

"Okay, let's go. Clearly this man does not want to sell. By the way, from the look of dust on it, I am sure it has sat here for a very long time."

"That's it, we're out of here." Gretchen grabbed her arm.

The doorbell chimed, and in came a tall man with a hat. He was not just any tall man in a hat. Gretchen took a second glance and yes, there he was, the cute rancher in the tight jeans and cowboy hat.

"Hey, Dad, how's it going?" Jennifer and Gretchen stopped right on cue and their jaws dropped.

"This is your dad?" they both chimed at exactly the same moment.

"Yup. Anything I can help you ladies with?" He was dripping with charm, and his drawl was right out of *Gone With the Wind*.

"Don't worry about it, son; these ladies do not know a fine item when they see one. They are offering only half the price for the only prize mantel clock in the store."

"Dad, remember where you got it?"

The girls could almost hear what he was saying. His southern drawl was not made for whispering.

"Yes, I know, the guy who sold it to me was young and had an accent. He was desperate to get a $100.00 for it and be gone."

"Okay, I will strike a bargain for you; I will take no less than $325.00, and that is my final offer."

Gretchen was the first to speak. "Take it, Jen. I will make up the difference."

"I can't do that. I will owe you."

Jennifer had her bank account balance in her head.

"Let's talk about this later. Right now you want to buy this item." Gretchen was stoic.

"It's now or never," said the store owner.

"I am closing in ten minutes."

"Oh, sure, that's interesting," queried Jennifer. "Your sign says you close at 5:00. It is now 4:20. Nice try!"

"We close early when it snows." The owner was impatient and dismissive at the same time. He left the area to serve another customer.

"Don't worry. I will take the sale. Please do not worry about my dad. He is old and cranky and has been in business for a long time. At the end of the day, he will be happy you paid the amount he wanted and not the full sale price."

"I am still not sure." Jennifer just wanted to leave.

"Come on, Jen. I know you want it." Gretchen was quick to respond. She was watching the snow outside and did not want to come back another day.

"What can I do to make you ladies feel happier about this? My name is Dustin, by the way. Happy to make your acquaintance."

"Gretchen here and my friend Jen." Gretchen was close to blinking her long eyelashes but realized it was too late for that. Dustin gave them motel business cards from the desk and then went to find his dad. After finding a pub for a tall drink and a hot meal, Gretchen phoned some of the numbers on the cards and they drove to a modest motel, where the price was affordable for both. Jennifer had a long bath and flopped into bed.

Gretchen showered and then sat up, reading. She could not get her mind off of the cowboy.

Wow, just think, a man like that to come home to every night, plus living on a ranch. Now I know why I told him where they worked; I would never have done that otherwise. Maybe one day he will roam into the bakery and have a coffee.

The next day, Gretchen and Jennifer picked up the mantel clock, paid for it, and drove home. On the way home, Gretchen told Jennifer everything she was thinking about the night before.

. . .

It was becoming dark, and Jennifer decided to start the stuffing. She was sure making it the night before would be best; she would just have to stuff the turkey in the morning and then prepare the potatoes and vegetables and keep an eye on the gravy. Misty, the maid her mom and dad employed when they were still together, taught her a lot about making Christmas dinner. The only problem was she had never really made one on her own.

The rice was cooked, and the Italian sausage for the stuffing was ready. Jennifer covered them both with sage and sautéed onion, and the house smelled wonderful. She left them to refrigerate until the morning.

Now the next best thing was to set the table for four. Even though Carlos had not phoned yet, she was going to be proactive and think positively—four it would be. She took down her best china and, after checking the tablecloth, put one plate on each side of the table. The cloth hung straight and was a sheer fabric—Christmas green. The plates were Royal Albert—traditional white with gold trim—and she enjoyed the beauty of these against the stark background. There were matching pickle dishes, vegetable dishes, salt and pepper, and a beautifully shaped gravy boat. She put out her best wine glasses and then her Christmas napkins and stood back to peruse the effect. She loved to decorate at home as well as at work. Jennifer dimmed the overhead lights, positioned tall silver candlestick holders, and inserted the dazzling Christmas candles in sparkly red, the ones that Misty gave her as a gift when she left. The phone rang; it was Carlos. He was able to attend, and he wanted to confirm the time. Dinner was at six. She tried not to sound like a little housewife or too excited that he was actually coming.

The rest of the evening went by quickly. She made a cheesecake for dessert and was pleased at how it looked: yummy, swimming with a glazed cherry top.

Jennifer slept well and was up early; she stuffed the turkey and put

Naked on the Inside

on some great music and relaxed. The day would be long and arduous but she was up for it. She was in between excited and nervous; she knew Carlos was coming, and she knew she had to remain a hostess for Freddie and Phillip. Jennifer was afraid she would look like she was swooning over Carlos, and that was her main worry. No, it was not the mistakes she might make cooking the lavish dinner; it was giving herself away with rampant feelings that made her body and thoughts become guarded.

As the day wore on, the dinner tasks started to take place of her feelings. She started the potatoes and the vegetables at 5:30. She took the perfectly done turkey out at 5:00 to let it rest before carving. *Just like the book says.* Jennifer could hear that line from a cooking show in her head.

Once the turkey was put on a holding rack, Jennifer drained the gravy drippings from the roasting pan and put them into a shallow pan on top of the stove for the next step. This she knew was a crucial step. She added the spices that Misty had taught her, to make the gravy tasteful but not too spicy, and then she shook a bottle with water and a thickener. Heating the gravy to a slow bubble, she added the thickener. Luckily she had the potatoes mashed and in the warming oven, as she needed all her focus for the gravy.

Just then the doorbell rang. It was Carlos. He had arrived almost fifteen minutes early, and she could see why. He had brought her the most exquisite bouquet of flowers she had ever seen. The bouquet was so big, she had to work fast to find a vase large enough to display them. She wanted some time with Carlos before her other guests arrived. Meanwhile, she turned the gravy down to the lowest heat level on the burner.

She had just put the flowers in the vase and placed them on the taller coffee table when she could feel a presence to her right. Carlos had followed her across the living room floor, and as soon as she lifted her head up from arranging the flowers he stole a kiss from her lips. Jennifer was so overwhelmed she barely heard the doorbell, and it was Carlos who answered. As he was letting in Freddie and Phillip, Jennifer had a chance to recoil and become the hostess she wanted to be.

75

13

Jennifer lit the candles on the table. She needed a distraction.

"Wow, it looks wonderful in here." Freddie was all praise and aglow with the magic a dinner conjures up.

"You have out done yourself." Phillip was also giving wonderful praises. "It smells fantastic."

Carlos was a great host. He started a conversation with the guys (as Jennifer called them), and then she had ample time to attend to the gravy and serve all of the dishes she had prepared ahead of time.

There were comments over the gravy and the stuffing and the whole dinner. Once the dessert was served, Jennifer felt as though all of the days of thinking and preparing for this special night were definitely worth it.

After the delicious cheesecake, Jennifer served coffee and then everyone retired to the living room. Jennifer loved the word "retired"; it sounded so sophisticated.

She thought it would be easy from that point on; the dinner was complete and everyone was full and happy. However, she did not notice what transpired after everyone sat down in the living room. She was just putting away the last of the food; she was thinking turkey sandwiches for lunches and was determined to keep the turkey covered to not dry out, when she saw Freddie go down on his knees.

"My clock, my clock." He was breathing rapidly, and she could barely hear him. Phillip and Carlos were trying to help him up off his knees. He would not budge.

"Jennifer, help us!" She could hear them almost screaming.

"What, what happened?" She was ready to call 911. She thought Freddie was having a heart attack.

"No, help us get him up and into the bedroom." Phillip was upset, and Jennifer had never seen him in this state.

"The clock, the clock." Freddie kept repeating the same phrase.

"What about the clock?" Jennifer was quite confused. "What about the clock?" She looked directly at Freddie, but he was quiet on the bed.

Freddie had passed out and was out for hours. They waited to see if he would wake up while they were there, but he did not.

"I will see you tomorrow." Carlos had to leave. He was feeling a little disappointed that he could not be with Jennifer the way he hoped he could be.

Phillip also had to leave. It was almost eleven o'clock P.M., and Freddie had not recovered from the shock of the clock. He was prostrate on Jennifer's bed in the main bedroom, but he was still breathing and sleeping comfortably.

Jennifer bade her company goodbye. She was just as puzzled as her other guests as to why Freddie was in such a state. She cleaned up the kitchen and ran the dishwasher. By this time it was almost midnight, so she had a long hot bath and found a pillow and enough blankets to cozy up on the couch with her cat, Sparky. She slept.

The next morning, she gave Freddie some coffee. This time it was in a ceramic cup, not a soft cup, and he left abruptly. There was no talking or no questions, and Jennifer felt a little hole in her heart over the results of the evening. It was still the Christmas holidays, and she was off for a few more days. Her mind went back to Freddie and his distress over the clock. It was very odd. The day was going to be long and lonely.

After her own breakfast, Jennifer was in a mess. She was lonely for Carlos and perplexed about Freddie. She had nobody to turn to, and when she phoned Gretchen she realized that it would not be fair to involve Gretchen with this new development during the holidays. She hung up before the call was answered. Little did she know that Gretchen was just as lonely as she was and hoping for the cute cowboy to phone. Of course, he would not be calling her residence; she had only told him about her workplace.

The snow was relentless. Jennifer watched it fall from her condo window with her cat, Sparky, on her lap. Every hour the snow piled higher on her windowsill and nameplate; it was too deep to back her car out. She was so glad she did not have to go to work; she pushed herself down onto her leather couch and read the day away. She loved Susan Isaacs and her style of writing. Her favorite book by her was called *Shining Through,* and she was rereading it this Christmas. She loved the movie with the same name with Melanie Griffith and Michael Douglas and how they played out this great film set in WWII.

Jennifer was almost asleep reading the book when she suddenly noticed there was a present under the tree. She sat up, went over to retrieve it, and found it to be labeled to herself from Freddie. He must have slid it under the tree when she was not looking the night before. He was so private and mysterious; she was glad she had not pressured him in the morning about his collapse the night before.

When she unwrapped the gift, she was absolutely stunned. She was standing in front of the tree but she had to sit down; her body was shaking. In the tiniest of boxes lay a necklace. It was absolutely beautiful, and a shock went through her whole body. It was a small diamond set into a medium-size flower shape. She turned it over, and there was an inscription on the back: "To a daughter I once had."

Jennifer ran to get a drink; she was so shocked at this new insight into Freddie's life, she had no words. What did this mean? What should she do now? She had no way to locate Freddie in this huge snowstorm. She chose not to phone him at the shelter. The thank-you would have to wait. She could invite him over alone another day or evening before the New Year, and hopefully he would share more of his past. Meanwhile, she handled the necklace with delicate fingers and put the box back under the tree.

. . .

Freddie had gone back to the shelter. He was aware of what happened the night before and felt badly he had startled everyone. There was no going back; it was what it was. He knew he would have to explain a couple of things to Jennifer and to her guests, but in some small part of his mind he was ready. He was ready to share his life and his past life. He knew the time would be right when it arrived, and this was the right time.

Meanwhile, he was concerned about Rick. He had not seen him lately and not only missed him but his dog, Ring. When Freddie followed his routine path to the bakery, he was quite surprised to see Rick and Ring out in the blizzard. Freddie put his hood over his head and smiled when he saw Rick.

"Merry Christmas." He greeted Rick with a warm hug.

Rick returned the hug, and then of course Ring was all over him. "I have nothing, boy, sorry."

Ring looked at him with sorrowful eyes and then started to nose his way through the snow pile beside him.

"How is it going, Rick, any new developments?"

"Well, we are still watching Latino Pizza. It looks a little suspicious but not enough to arrest anyone. We are waiting for them to move or make a mistake. Ring senses something is unusual, and I certainly do as well. By the way, how was Christmas dinner? Did you enjoy being at Jennifer's? Was Carlos on his best behavior?"

"Carlos was a gentleman. Phillip was also a gentleman. There is no accounting for taste. Jennifer made a grand meal, and we all had a wonderful time." Freddie voiced this shyly. Little did Rick know that Freddie was only telling part of the story; he did not mention the part where he fainted and had to be carried to Jennifer's bedroom for the rest of the evening.

14

It was late in the afternoon the first week after the New Year, and most of the employees had gone home. Carlos was curious about the man who delivered pizza to his house a few weeks ago. He wandered into the lower part of the huge house and saw that it had many rooms. He rang the bell at the front, and the person who answered was the man who looked very much like him.

"Hi, I know you probably do not have a lot of walk in traffic and it is still the holidays, but I was so curious about you that I had to come in." Carlos felt like an intruder.

"Hi, my name is Fernando. I work here and I own part of the business. My uncle is the full owner, and he is in the back. It has been on my mind also that you look very similar; I do not know why, but I was thinking that I would ask my uncle. " Fernando was full of manners and wanted to make Carlos feel comfortable, so he shook his hand.

When Fernando asked his uncle to come to the front, he came with his apron on and his hands held many vegetables. He was cutting and preparing pizza for a party that night and not able to talk for a long time.

When Carlos saw him, he took a step back. He had no idea he would see the same man he saw in the picture with his sister. He could not believe it, so he took a respectful approach. He introduced himself and also shook his hand.

"Hi, my name is Carlos and my sister had photos of you at our house."

The owner with white hair dismissed himself and went to the back room. He said nothing of the sister and nothing else except, "Nice to meet you."

Carlos knew he had to come back another day. He wanted Rick to be with him and to ask questions. There was something odd about it all, and he knew with the photos he could prove something. Meanwhile, he would bide his time until the holiday season was over.

• • •

When Carlos arrived at Jennifer's condo unannounced, Jennifer breathed deeply. She was excited and happy all at the same time. The first thing Jennifer did was show Carlos what Freddie had bought her. She was lucky that Carlos was not the jealous type but preferred to think of the gift as something a compassionate older friend would offer.

He was not sure of the inscription or what it meant, but these things did not bother Carlos. His life in Colombia was so different, he had no words to explain it. Poverty made a person feel differently, and it made a person see things differently. He was glad for Jennifer but had no idea as to the value of the necklace.

Jennifer wanted to spend time with Carlos and not cook, so she ordered a pizza. When Carlos found out that Jennifer had ordered a pizza from Latino Pizza, he was curious to see who would deliver it. When Fernando showed up, Carlos wanted to see Jennifer's response to their similarities.

After Carlos paid him and closed the door, Jennifer was all radar.

"Did you see how he looked like you? Rick kept showing me a picture when the robberies happened and was convinced it was you, but it was not. Now I am curious. Who is this guy?"

Carlos was as confused as Jennifer by the similarity and had been for a long time. Over the last month, he had been trying to contact his aunt and uncle but to no avail. They were still not at their previous home address. He was hoping they would give him some answers as to the incredible similarities. Then an idea became solid in Carlos's head: What if he showed a picture of his aunt and uncle to Fernando and then to his boss (the man with the white hair)? Would they recognize his aunt and uncle as anyone they knew from the past?

• • •

It was January 15, and Rick was on the street with Ring. Carlos was running through the crisp snow and frigid temperatures. Rick saw him first and could not understand how runners stood the cold frigid air in their lungs.

"Hey, Rick, do you have time for a coffee?"

Carlos stopped right in front of the security station and was just heading east. Ring was all ears when Carlos pet him and continued to sniff his trousers and pockets.

"He is still looking for a lead." Rick was all business. "Once again he was given the scent of the last robbery, and we are off today. The cold doesn't help, but Ring is highly trained and maybe today is the day he will detect a scent and hopefully we will have some data for the robberies and murder...."

"I will meet you at the bakery when you're done, Rick."

"Talk soon." Rick was literally being pulled by Ring in another direction. There was something out there, and Ring was determined to scout it out.

85

After what seemed like an hour later, Rick arrived at the bakery with Ring in tow. They had been running hard, and Ring was more than happy to be tied to the bicycle rack while Rick went inside for something warm.

"Hey, how's our valiant detective?" Jennifer had rosy cheeks from the warmth of the bakery and offered Rick coffee from the globe of a freshly perked coffee pot.

"Not so much happening lately," Rick confessed.

"Carlos and I were wondering how you came to have a photo of a man who was attached to the robberies." Jennifer kept pouring.

"A proud citizen took the photo outside the home that was robbed. He took it on his cell phone and then offered it to us at the police station. There is no proof the man is the robber; he was just in the vicinity. He was running and that was why we were suspicious of runners that day." Rick stated this fact with an apologetic air; he knew how Jennifer felt about Carlos.

"Have you seen the man who delivers for Latino Pizza? He looks so much like Carlos, he could be his twin." Jennifer wanted Rick to know this.

"Freddie has been watching the site, but I have not met the man close up." Rick knew there was another lead ready to work on, but he was waiting for the right time.

After Carlos arrived and coffee and cinnamon buns were served, Rick and Carlos decided to meet in two days to talk to Fernando.

Meanwhile, Rick untied Ring and left the bakery to climb to the commercial area where signs were sold. The snow was brilliant with tiny bursts of crystals that looked like buried diamonds. Ring found the easy way up, and the view was breathtaking. Rick stopped to catch his breath and nuzzled Ring behind his ears.

"Good boy."

Once he reached the top, Rick found a bicycle rack to tie him and then opened the door to Magnetic Signs. The front desk showed numerous examples of sign choices, and Rick was looking for the one he saw on the van.

"Would you mind if I looked at that sign more closely?" Rick pointed to one high up on the wall.

The sales clerk climbed a ladder and brought the sign down. "No problem. Is there anything else I can help you with today?"

Rick turned the sign over and asked a couple of questions as to the magnetic aspect of the sign and if it was able to be on one van and then able to be taken off and put onto another van.

When Rick showed his detective badge, the clerk was startled. He went back to get his boss. When his boss arrived, Rick was adamant about asking if a company called Latino Pizza had bought the sign he was looking at.

The boss retrieved his files and responded, "Yes, this sign was bought by Latino Pizza one month ago, and it is transferable to any van or company vehicle. They had their business name put on it with red and white colors, as well as an artist's rendition of a pizza slice."

15

Freddie phoned and found Jennifer home on a Saturday toward the end of January. Previous to this, he could not muster up enough courage to walk into the bakery and face Jennifer. He was devastated with his behavior and felt as though he had ruined her Christmas dinner. "Freddie. Oh, my, I could not stop thinking about you. You have been on my mind at work and at home every day since Christmas. How have you been? Come, come over, I need to see you."

When Freddie walked the long distance to Jennifer's condo, his shoulders were full of snow and he was coughing. Jennifer made him sit and take off his wet outer clothing, and then she made him a hot drink.

He looked at her again like the daughter he once had and smiled and felt warm in his heart—so warm that his eyes were moistening up and he had to look away. Jennifer was scurrying around in the kitchen for snacks and another drink. This time it was one with rum in it.

"Thank you, my darling. You have no idea what you mean to me."

Jennifer had an idea how much she meant to him. She took the necklace from under the tree, unwrapped it, and held it up between her fingers right in front of the window, and it sparkled with the late afternoon sun shining right on the diamond.

She turned and looked at Freddie. "Thank you from the bottom of my heart. You have no idea how much this meant to me when I unwrapped it. What does it mean when it says 'To a daughter I once had'?"

Freddie said, "Do you have a couple of hours? I would like to tell you about my life and tell you what I have lost."

Jennifer felt her heart jump in her chest; she knew this day would come, and she was ready. "Yes, I have all afternoon, Freddie. As a matter of fact, I will take some turkey and gravy out of the freezer from Christmas dinner, and you will enjoy dinner with me later. I am ready, my friend, to hear your story."

Freddie sipped his hot drink with rum; he was feeling warmer not just on the outside, but his insides were warming up to the point where he was taking off his sweater and then he settled in. He found a spot on the couch and a coaster for his drink, and then he started to speak. Much to Jennifer's amazement, he was a decorated journalist. She had no idea. Her jaw dropped each time he mentioned something new in his past. He reiterated the news broadcasts he wrote about and the national and international stories he was involved in from Europe to Asia to the Americas. He brought up topics in the news from years back that she as a young student in high school remembered her teacher talking about, and then he stopped.

Jennifer waited and then Freddie sat very still. He had tears in his eyes, and he could not go on. Jennifer then got up and went to the fridge and served him a colossal piece of cheesecake swimming with cherry topping.

Freddie ate and felt revitalized, and then he continued. "One day when many of my dangerous journalist experiences were over, I went home for lunch. At the time, I had a beautiful young wife and a eight-year-old daughter. To this day, no one knows why or how but they were both swimming in blood when I arrived home that fateful afternoon. My life has never been the same, and it never will be. I do not know how I survived it all. If it was not for my very close friend Phillip,

I would have taken my own life. To this day, all of the CIA, detectives, and crime scene teams have not been able to find the killer or killers. I was devastated. I quit my job. I have been under the bridge as a homeless man for ten years now, and my life has taken a 360-degree turn. My daughter would be approximately your age this day. Therefore, I must tell you that even though she was young I know she would have grown up to be kind and sweet like you, helping the homeless and going to bat, so to speak, for others who are less fortunate."

Jennifer's eyes were moist with tears, and she quietly got up to start dinner for the two of them.

Over dinner Jennifer heard more details of Freddie's past. He continued on to go further back into history and talk of his father and grandfather. He adored both of them and talked of his grandfather's skills of being a watchmaker and how he had an incredulous business during the war. He would offer credit to all of his patrons knowing he could barely feed his own family. He lived in a two-story house in Amsterdam, and his workshop was on the bottom floor of his house while his family lived upstairs. He knew the Nazis were confiscating everything in Holland, including precious art pieces and anything of value.

Jan, his grandfather, had a specialized skill in making clocks. He would sit up nights making lavish mantel clocks that patrons of the time would purchase, then exhibit on their elaborate mantels.

One day a Dutch businessman entered his store. The bell rang at the front door at street level, and Jan went down to greet him. This man knew what the Germans were doing; they were confiscating any art they could get their hands on, including anything of value. He had a mantel clock that my grandfather had made him just a year prior. In it he said he had hidden a key. The key was to a safe place in Holland that he was sure no one could find. With this key, only an informed finder would be able to recognize the station (train station) that the key would fit and then the locker.

The key held the answer. Inside the locker that the key unlocked was a description of numerous art pieces held by the Dutchman. The art was hidden under floorboards in a specific building in the city that he was sure once again the Germans could not find.

Many years after the war, the art and valuables were being sought after to be returned to Holland. When national and international news spread, many tried to find a way to get their hands on this wealth. At one time, there was speculation that all of the clocks were pieces of mystery.

"When it was told that I had a valuable item from my Dutch inheritance, numerous phone calls came to my house. I had no idea there may be a key in the mantel clock. I defied any accusation of that truth, and finally the phone calls stopped. There was no way I was going to take the clock apart to appease some greedy nosy people who lived on other people's inheritance. The clock sat on my mantel for a very long time. One day when she was older, I was going to inform my daughter and tell her the beautiful history behind the clock and, of course, tell her of my father and grandfather and all about Holland. The chance never came; she was killed at such a young age. I froze the past behind me and never wanted to look back."

16

It was the third week in January, and Carlos and Rick found themselves at the same place. Rick pushed the bell this time with his palm, and out came Fernando from the back, wiping his hands.

"Wow, this is a great place, almost as big as a warehouse." Rick was so overwhelmed by the fact that Fernando looked like the twin of Carlos, he had to say something to distract himself. "So, Fernando, is it…. Do you run?"

"Ya, sure, sometimes I do." He looked perplexed.

"Is this you in this picture?" Rick pulled the picture from the folio he had in his hands.

"Ya, sure, that is a shirt I wear when I run. It has number 24 on it, and it is a bright orange. I love that shirt; it reminds me of a team I watch on TV." Fernando was beginning to suspect. He looked up and there it was, a detective's badge staring him in the face. "What is this? I did nothing wrong."

"There was a robbery close to where you were running that day. A man was out on his lawn, and he took this picture with his phone just when you were running by. He was actually taking pictures of his new car, but he got you as well. Shortly after that, the police were called, as there was a robbery on the same street."

Rick did not mention there was murder as well. He was very intent on watching the face of Fernando for any recognition or fear about being in the same vicinity as a police scene. He showed neither fear, remorse, nor interest.

It was also the murder of the sister of Carlos. Carlos was reading the numerous pizza choices on the end wall of the pizza front and not in ear shot. Rick was glad because he wanted to question Fernando on his own.

"Did you hear on the news that day that there was a robbery and also a murder?" Rick kept watching his face closely.

Meanwhile, Ring was sitting patiently the whole time and at times wiggling his nose at the great smells coming from the back room.

Fernando had gone white. He could not believe he was not only being told of a robbery but now a murder. "I do not know of a murder." His hands started to shake a little, and he became quite distracted.

Carlos arrived at the counter in time to see the change in his face. He saw Fernando go from nonchalant, to friendly, to looking white and placid. He decided to ask if his boss was in. Fernando was glad for the distraction; he went back to get his boss one more time.

"I want you to see his boss," he said to Rick. "I want you to know that my sister has pictures of him in our house. The fact that she was murdered and has pictures of him—someone I had never met—makes me very suspicious." Carlos was starting to whisper as another person appeared at the counter.

After Rick and the owner met, there was not much Rick could say. He was hesitant to start a conversation with him. He would look at the pictures Carlos had first with his sister and then determine another approach. He was glad he had met him and saw what he looked like. His name was Owen Nanchez, and he was the uncle of Fernando.

. . .

Carlos and Rick left Latino Pizza, taking Ring with them after Fernando gave him a piece of pizza crust.

"Fernando will be his friend forever," Rick was mumbling as he left perplexed about everything.

Not only had they been watching Latino Pizza for a long time, but now there was a friendly face that worked there who looked exactly like Carlos. Also, Ring was not even close to smelling anything that would help the investigation.

Rick met Carlos at his house to look at the pictures. There was still a chance something would show up in them that would make everything seem clearer. When Rick saw the picture of Owen, the boss of Latino Pizza, he had no doubt this was the same man. The only problem he was having was convincing Carlos that, yes, his sister could have been seeing him for a while before he arrived in Canada. The only suspicious thing about it was she did not mention him.

It looked as though the sister was so much younger that she could have been the daughter, not the girlfriend, the way the picture imaged.

"Do you have any others?" Rick was curious now, and the few he was looking at were all in the same area, outside and very close up. In one he was kissing her on the lips, so ruling out the daughter aspect was probably quite right.

Carlos looked in the same closet and looked on the floor in case something had fallen out. There was nothing.

"I just cannot understand why she never talked about him. Maybe he gave her money and helped her when she first arrived. I would be glad to know anything to help me find the murderer who took her life. I had trouble with her bossy personality, but I will not forget how she phoned my aunt and uncle in Colombia and fought to get money for my whole first year of university."

Carlos was distraught over the whole incident being brought up again, and he threw himself on the couch in a slouching manner.

"Let me take these down to the lab." Rick was adamant that there must be something in one of the pictures that might give a clue. "If the lab blows them up, we may find something on a wall or on their person that will help." Rick was being positive, as he could see the absolute desolation in Carlos.

17

Jennifer knew the story was real and it gave her a sad, empty feeling in the pit of her stomach. She knew he was not looking for pity, so she made a clear attempt to start dinner to distract him. It was the worst story she had ever heard. It touched her deeply, so deeply she knew she would not sleep for a long time; her heart ached for Freddie in the worst way, worse than any other event in her life, including her parents splitting up, and the last day Misty, her confidante and friend, made the last meal in her parents' house.

Walking over to the tree, Jennifer once again saw the small gift Freddie had given her and felt stricken with grief that this gift was not able to be given to his rightful daughter. At the same time, Jennifer could feel her heartstrings pulling for the tenderness that came with the gift. The fact that he gave the gift to her touched her so deeply, tears welled up in her eyes much like the first time she opened it. Freddie had followed her over to the tree. When she looked up at him, he could see her distress and once again he pulled out his plaid handkerchief and offered it to her.

"Is it clean?" she queried with a slight smile.

"Yes, my dear, done at the shelter laundry."

It was then Freddie slowly put his arm around her shoulder and waited. He waited just long enough and finally she turned around, stepped into him, and lay her head on his shoulder. She sobbed. She sobbed slowly at first and then uncontrollably. Freddie stood very still. He knew she was sobbing for him and for his lost wife and daughter. She was sobbing for the situation, the sadness, and the loneliness.

Once Jennifer started to relax, she stepped back and saw that the light in Freddie's eyes had changed. He stood taller and somehow he looked younger. It was as though a huge weight had been lifted from him, and he breathed deeply.

Just then the oven bell went off, and dinner was ready. Jennifer knew it was time to serve the Christmas turkey and gravy she had reheated for tonight. She pulled out a salad and microwaved the potatoes. All this time Freddie was not in the kitchen; he was standing very still in the living room.

Sliding herself slowly over to the area of the fireplace, she watched. There was a slowness in his movements. She noticed the clock was not on the mantel; it was in his hands. He was turning it over and over as if in disbelief. He stopped turning it when he had the bottom of it turned up once again.

Jennifer continued to watch; she could see his stance. He was frozen in space; his hands were not moving, his head hung down. His large body took on a new look as if he was immortalized as a statue. For the first time she noticed his dark green corduroy shirt, his taupe-coloured pants, and his shoulder-length tawny-coloured hair. His belt gave away the breadth of his waist, and he was indeed a large man. His stance did not last for a long time; it was in the way he moved next that made her mouth drop and her body become motionless. What Jennifer saw next was a man going back in time in his spirit and soul. He ran his hand over the bottom right of the mantel clock. What he saw there Jennifer remembered when she purchased the clock. He made no movement until his fingers moved lovingly and gently over the letters that were engraved on the metal bottom. Jennifer remembered these letters; she had seen them, but at the time of the purchase they meant nothing to her.

Freddie was mumbling to himself, "It really is my grandfather's clock; it really is. Here are his initials right here – JVS. Look, Jen."

Jennifer had never heard him call her Jen before, so she knew he was on a different plane of emotion right now. She was ecstatic that he was excited.

Jennifer moved over to the fireplace and sidled up to Freddie's right arm; he motioned for her to look at the initials and then went on to tell his story.

"My grandfather, bless his heart, was in my life for a long time. He was a large part of my childhood and was there for me in his shop whenever I wanted to talk with him. His beautiful quaint shop ticked with all kinds of clocks and watches. The walls were full of the most exquisite clock faces that Holland had to offer. My father and grandfather were known for their mastery in clock making and in clock repair. My father was an excellent clock master, but my grandfather had a skill that could not be found anywhere. The little bell on the door of the shop would indicate a customer and even at noon, when my grandfather was upstairs having soup, he would interrupt his meal and almost bounce down the stairs to help a customer. He kept in great shape because he would always be the one to offer a personal delivery on his bike. Unlike here, bicycles were rampant in Holland and used for everyday transportation around the city by workers alike."

Jennifer stood very still while Freddie was telling his story. She could hear the microwave bell, knowing the potatoes were done; however, she chose to not move a muscle. For many months now she wanted Freddie to tell her of his past, and now he had opened up like a flower, petal by petal.

Jennifer did not want to interrupt Freddie, but she could not wait until he told her what the initials meant. She knew they were a name, but what was the name?

It was as though he had read her mind.

"The name on the clock should have been in full, but my grandfather chose this simpler version to save time. There were numerous men in Holland with the name Jan. There were also clockmakers with the last name van Stralen. Amazingly, Dutch clockmakers were not in competition with each other; they helped each other when a customer could not find what they needed. "

"But how would they know this came from your grandfather's workshop and not another if the same initials were inscribed from another shop owner?" Jennifer was becoming more curious now, and it was a good time to ask questions.

"There was an unsaid code that each shop owner would use a different script, or today it would be called font. My grandfather chose this very simple broad-stroked block style, but if you look closely you will see that there is a slight curl to the beginning and end of each letter. It is so faint that it is only able to be discerned with a magnifying glass."

"Oh, Freddie , I have one." Jennifer ran to her garden tool jar and found it. "I use it to read seed packages."

Freddie gingerly took it from Jennifer's hands, and they looked at the letters together. Jennifer was amazed at how with a little magnification all the letters showed a slight curl.

Freddie stopped and then sat down. He looked a little white, and then he had tears in his eyes. "This really is my grandfather's, and I cannot believe it. What are the chances that after ten years of looking, a nearby store puts it on the shelf and then a very dear friend of mine, meaning you, my dear, buys it?"

"I call it fate." Jennifer had read and seen strange phenomena in her young life, so this was not impossible to understand. She had once heard Misty talk about how two identical brothers were separated at birth and then with different adoptive families came to live in America, and their families ended up living two blocks from each other. It wasn't until the boys went to school that the families discovered the lookalike boys and when they were registered in the same school and the same class the parents just had to meet.

Freddie was very interested in Jennifer's story. *Maybe it is fate. However, it does make me wonder how the clock came to be in an antique store close by.* "Jennifer, where did you buy it?"

"I bought it in Vernon. The man who sold it to me said he had it for a long time. It was full of dust, and the label on it was for a lot of money. I paid over three hundred for it, but he was adamant at the time for the full price. I was really tired that day, and if it wasn't for Gretchen pulling me away I probably would have punched the owner; he was very cranky. We did hear him say, however, that a man with an accent sold it to him originally and after getting one hundred dollars for it basically ran out of the store."

"We have to go to that store, Jennifer; we just have to."

Jennifer had never seen Freddie so adamant or so animated. His demure was slow, sad, and steady on the best of days. She wanted to think about all the facts that Freddie had related to her for a while before driving back to the store in Vernon in the snow.

Freddie was interested in going to the store and voiced his request, but something in the way Jennifer described the clock made his mind go back to his grandfather's shop.

He remembered as a little boy his father telling him about his grandfather. All of the elder clockmakers in Holland were having a meeting. They knew something very serious in all of the lives of the people in Holland was about to happen with the invasion; it was somewhere between 1940 and 1941.

Many elders had relatives and numerous friends, as well as customers, who were beginning to see what was ahead regarding the war. Customers especially were becoming increasingly worried about the nature of the war and what this meant to Amsterdam. There was talk of rich families having their houses taken away—expropriated—and the worry was fast rising.

"One night," Freddie said, "his dad overheard his grandfather talking to other watchmakers in Holland. All of the watchmakers wanted to help their rich friends hide their wealth. Hans, a very diligent man in business, mentioned we must ship all the wealth out of the country so the Germans will not get their hands on any of it. Hans was right. In the end, all the wealth in Amsterdam was taken; however, some artwork and other items were sent to America to be hidden and safely stored away.

"Father went on to say that he knew of families later who found their treasures due to an extremely clever plan that was fashioned by all of the men at that meeting. These men decided to not only hide their art but hide the keys that would find their art."

"No, they did not hide all of the keys in clocks, did they?" Jennifer was hypnotized with excitement.

"Yes, the ingenious plan of Hans worked extremely well. He masterminded a system where specific clocks from random shops held a key. This was done so the Germans would not figure out the pattern. There are three clocks left according to the records that were kept. This is one of them."

"How do you know, Freddie? Where is the record?" Jennifer forgot about the dinner, the potatoes, and anything else in the room. She was immediately fascinated by Freddie's story.

"Most of the records have been handed down through the generations of Dutch clockmakers. It was not a good idea to give it up to any war museum. I only know there were three left from the information my father left me before he died. However, the other two may have been found by now, but I have a feeling I would have been informed of this."

"How would you have been informed?" Jennifer was intrigued by this story and needed to know more.

"There is a secret system the elder clockmakers use to this day—passed down through the generations. I do not know it, as I chose not to become a clock maker or watch repair proprietor. Therefore, if I had this clock opened and if there was a key in it, I would not know where to look for the use of it. The code for finding the compartment is intrinsic and memorized by the remaining few. If there was a key in this mantel clock, I would be doing some incredible research of my ancestors to find out what container or warehouse the key would fit."

"That is it, Freddie. The thief or thieves took only this clock and nothing else from your house. They must have known about the key." Jennifer was setting up a good scenario, but then she stopped.

"If they knew about the key in the clock and the plan where it may fit a warehouse full of priceless art, why would they sell it to an antique store for only one hundred dollars?" Freddie was fast in his reply.

Jennifer realized this was why she stopped. "It does not make sense. The fact that your wife and daughter were killed and this clock was taken and then sold makes no sense at all. Of course the thief may have known police were looking for it. The fact that it was not picked up later makes me believe that the thief had no idea what it contained. It was just a beautiful object, shiny and expensive, that would bring a good price."

"I will have the clock opened, and we will know for sure what it contains. I also want it dusted for fingerprints; the slim chance of finding a print on it is practically nil, especially one that matches the half-print on the counter at the crime scene." Freddie felt as though he was repeating himself, but it kept the possibility alive.

Jennifer went over, took the clock out of Freddie's hands, and carefully put it back on the mantel. She tenderly took Freddie by the elbow and sat him down at the table. The warmed-up dinner was cooler than expected, but Jennifer gave Freddie a hot drink and he looked as though he was relaxed. She turned the lights down so his eyes could rest. She served him up a turkey dinner, and he felt gratitude again for this lovely young girl who had taken him under her wing and given him hope, strength, love, and a warm spirit to carry him through the rest of his years.

Freddie could feel the warm tears dwelling in his eyes again, and he had to have full control of his faculties to force himself to stop crying and to look at Jennifer. She smiled back at him with a warm heart, sparkle in her eyes, and the look that a father would receive if his real daughter were there.

"Don't forget that we have all the hope in the world with the clock. We may find a key, and we may find a fingerprint. Freddie, imagine if we found at least one of these." Jennifer became very animated.

"That would be more than I could ever hope for…but right now some cherry cheesecake would be nice."

18

The phone rang, and Rick's wife answered it. She was up early planning units for her work, and she called Rick from the bedroom.

"It's for you, Officer Cliff."

"We have something. The bakery van was seen early this morning around two A.M. loading up at Latino's."

"Who reported?" Rick's first question. "I will kiss his butt."

"I think I will put him on the payroll. None other than your lofty homeless friend Freddie. " Officer Cliff laughed. "Told you we would use him...."

Rick was more than happy. Once he said goodbye to Officer Cliff, stating he would be down in a half-hour, he ran over to Ring and nuzzled his ears. "Let's go, boy." He related all the good on the phone to his wife and, grabbing Ring's leash, he raced out the door.

The run today was pure and magnificent. The air was like the Arctic, and there was nothing more beautiful than a winter morning in the interior of British Columbia. The sky was blue, and everything was crystallized as though a magic wand had transported the surroundings into a fairyland. Rick kept running, and Ring kept up to his even faster pace. They ran together, both harmonizing with the same stride, the same rhythm, the same purpose.

When Rick ran past the bakery and then Latino's, absolutely nothing looked different. Except for the sign dropping off the bakery truck the night before, they had not made one mistake. Now, they had. This was the break they were waiting for. Rick was exuberant as he breathlessly strode into the station.

"Hey, Officer Cliff, good job." Rick saluted him in the fun way he did.

"The credit goes to your friend Freddie; he was our ace in the hole."

"Ya, what's he worth on your payroll?" Rick leashed up Ring who, at this time, was walking around proudly with his tail up, sensing all the excitement.

Officer Cliff called a meeting, and all of the officers agreed this was high priority. The machines were going fast, and all of the lights were on. Data was coming in from Vancouver and stats on the alleged drug scheme coming through none other than the Interior city.

19

Freddie was very upset about how he handled himself at the Christmas dinner. There was a sadness in his heart that he could not dismiss; it would not go away, causing him to have trouble sleeping. There was no way he was ever going to forget what he saw in Jennifer's living room that night. When he saw the mantel clock sitting sedately on the fireplace shelf, he was distraught. For ten years now, he had realized the chances of finding his mantel clock would be slim, if at all. Now that he saw the item he had been missing for so long in the living room of one of his closest friends, he could not forget it. Who was she, and how did she get his clock? There was no mistaking that Jennifer was innocent; she had no idea what she had there. What Freddie wanted to know was exactly where she purchased it, what store, what city, and who originally sold it to the store owner. He was also curious as to how much she had paid for it. Even if he had the answers to half of these questions, it would give him some peace of mind. He was also convinced that the purchase was made in another city; he had looked forever in all of the shops in the immediate area. He knew any city within driving distance and any antique or second-hand store within these limits held no such item. He knew this because his mission during the early years was to find that clock.

Freddie kept climbing the hill to Jennifer's condo, and his mind was continually active; it would not shut off. There was no way he was going to blame her or inflict accusations; she had no idea about this clock, and she certainly did not know its past. All he could think about was how much he loved her like the daughter he once had. He was also thinking about the gift he had inadvertently slipped under the tree for her that night. He hoped that she delighted in it just like his own daughter would have if she had lived.

Freddie was panting now as he approached the summit of the hill. He could see Jennifer's condo as he rose over the last incline. He was happy that he had finally arrived, but he was also apprehensive to face her. There was so much at stake. He knew he would have to explain everything, not just his behaviour at the dinner but his current life and his past life so it would all make sense to her.

Now he was at the front door; he could see her nameplate, "Jennifer Shields," half hidden by snow. The mounting snow on her front porch and driveway was a measurable indication of the amount of snow that had fallen over the last few nights.

The doorbell was right there, but Freddie could not push the bell. If it wasn't for Jennifer opening the door to greet him, he may not have conjured up the courage. When Jennifer saw him, she looked at him square in the face and he just froze. When he would not move toward her, she stepped over into his personal space and gave him a huge hug.

Freddie teared up, hugged her back, and kept repeating, "I'm sorry, I'm sorry." Jennifer drew him into the warm embrace of her condo and sat him down on the couch. She retrieved a blanket from the back room and covered his knees. He smiled at her with a large smile while she hustled herself to the kitchen to make him a hot sweet drink.

Freddie sat very still; he could not or dare not move. He was not quite sure which at this particular moment. He could not move due to his legs being tingly and warm right now, and he dare not move for fear of what he may say to Jennifer without thinking it out first. The last thing he wanted was for her to feel blamed about something she had no idea about until he explained everything else perfectly.

She was so sweet, and she really looked after him. There was no one more loving or more real in his life right now; no one who made it as meaningful or as rich as Jennifer. There she was in the kitchen, hustling to make him a hot drink on a cold January day. *What else would his daughter do?* he thought. *There is no other way to show love than hugging someone or doing something very special for them.*

Jennifer was filling the coffee mugs with a sweet drink Misty had taught her to make. She waited until Jennifer was late into her teens to show her how to make the one with anisette, a liqueur that tasted like licorice. When Jennifer turned to see how Freddie was doing, she saw him with his head dropped to his chest and he was staring at his knees. *He looks so sad*, she thought. *I just do not know where to begin when I talk to him. I hope he starts first and then I will be the listener.* She felt like listening today; she was waiting for answers, and she hoped they would find their way into the conversation.

When Jennifer put the drinks on the coffee table, Freddie said a very soft "thank you," almost inaudible. She watched him sip slowly and then put the mug down.

He looked at her with filled eyes—full of love and close to brimming with tears. "Thank you kindly."

He extended his arm to touch her shoulder, and she felt as though her father was right in the room with her. Just thinking about him also was enough to bring tears to her own eyes.

"You're welcome, so very much." Jennifer reached across and gave him a very slight kiss on the forehead.

It was then that Freddie turned to Jell-O and he lost all resolve. The tears started to fall, and as they slid down his cheek he was starting to shake and then he was crying uncontrollably. "You are so kind," he said, and as Jennifer was reaching for a tissue Freddie knew it was going to be a long night.

He cried into the tissue for a long time, and Jennifer waited. Then Freddie wiped his eyes with his plaid handkerchief, and he sat up straight. He took a long sip of his drink, and there was warmth in his cheeks and a look of heightened awareness when he put his mug down.

"Where do I begin?" He was not sure how to start. He needed help to know where to start. He needed to know that she would be there through his whole speech; he felt as though it was going to be a speech—his whole life a speech.

Jennifer was young but extremely insightful. She knew Freddie was struggling with everything he wanted to say. She knew she was going to have to help him.

"Tell me about the clock, Freddie." Jennifer knew that starting with the present day was a good idea; she learned this from a counselor she saw once a week when she was distraught from her parents' breakup. She was hoping he would go back in time and fill in the blanks later. So that was exactly where Freddie started, with the present day.

"The clock, Jennifer, is a family heirloom." Being a journalist in his past, Freddie knew the importance of fact, not emotion. He decided to talk like a journalist so she would understand the facts first, and this would also deflect him from breaking down during highly emotional moments. "My grandfather made this clock in Holland before the war. He was a well-renowned clockmaker, and his initials are probably on this clock. Yes, here it is." Freddie had stood up and wandered over to the fireplace mantel and, turning the clock upside down, he read the engraved initials: JvS – Jan van Stralen – his grandfather's full Dutch name.

"How did you know they were there?" Jennifer was mystified as to how he would have identified it so quickly.

"I saw them the night of the Christmas dinner. I was just putting your gift under the tree, and something inside me knew this clock had special meaning. It was calling me to look at it and calling me to turn it over. I was lucky that night that I was here and had a place to lie down and crash—so to speak. If I had seen this clock in a store, I am sure I would have fallen to the floor and the staff would have had to call 911. So thank you, Jennifer, for being the one who purchased the clock and that it is in the hands of one of the most important people in my life."

"Thank you for the beautiful Christmas gift, Freddie. I will cherish it forever, but I do not understand the inscription. 'To the daughter I once had.' Did you have a daughter?"

"Yes, I had a daughter." Freddie took a long sip of the cooled-off drink, sat back on the couch, and made himself comfortable so he could start his story. "Many years ago, I had a daughter and she would be approximately your age today. She was murdered along with her mother in a robbery/murder that happened long ago. The person or persons who committed this crime were never caught, so I have lived with this for more than ten years now and all the while searching for the one item that was stolen during the robbery. The clock on my mantel at the time was the same clock sitting here. I was hoping to find it with a fingerprint on it, a fingerprint that would match the half-fingerprint that was found on the counter at the house during the crime scene."

Freddie went on to tell Jennifer about the clock that was given to him. He went back in time to paint a visual picture for Jennifer about his life as a young boy in Holland. His name was Frederick van Stralen, sitting with the same last name as his grandfather. His life, he said, was easy, fun, and full of love. He rode his bicycle everywhere, but he chose to change his life as a young adult. He wanted to see the world, and so he came to Canada. He became intrigued with worldly news and then trained in Toronto to be a journalist. He met his wife during university, and once their child was born she stayed home and loved it. Her life as a journalist before they met took her to many countries, and she loved to travel as he did. Later in their careers, the job became increasingly dangerous.

"Who would know the real danger for her was just being at home that particular day?" Freddie looked up while he said this, and his eyes were glassy with tears. "It seems so unfair, so many lives cut short by others who think they have the right to take them."

Jennifer sat paralyzed by this; she knew the same thing had happened to Carlos. His loss was great as well. He had lost his mom and dad early in life, and just when he had moved to a new country much like Freddie, he lost another person close to him. His sister was murdered right here, and as far as she knew the person responsible for this crime had not been caught.

"Do you feel as though moving away from your birthplace was the best idea, Freddie, or do you wish you still lived in Holland?" Jennifer was not sure if she could ever move from Canada and actually live in another country—visit, maybe, but not live.

"You are young, Jennifer, and so was I at the time; however, Europe was changing and I felt free when I travelled. So here I am. I am glad that I have you; you mean a lot to me. You have helped me through these last months when life under the bridge was becoming unbearable with nobody in my life to give it meaning or make it rich. You have done that, my dear, and I am so grateful for what you have done for me being the old guy I am."

Jennifer squealed with laughter. "You will never be old, Freddie."

Freddie kept looking at the fireplace, and his eyes focused directly on the clock once again. His mind went back in time, and he was transported back to Holland. He could see the shop, the clocks, the customers. He could feel the presence of his grandfather, feel his love, sense the joy in his heart whenever his hands created something. He saw his own father sitting right beside him, and then he saw his mother and grandmother upstairs in the kitchen making delicious little cakes and serving them on frilly white doilies. It was then Freddie wondered why he had left; he could hear what Jennifer was saying. *Maybe it was not a good idea to meander into another country and leave behind a well-worn heritage and generations of relatives.*

Freddie rose and went over to the clock. He lifted it off the mantel and then looked at Jennifer with a query on his mind.

Jennifer watched him closely and knew he was thinking very deeply about something. "What is it, Freddie?"

"I was just thinking...would you let me take the clock for a short time, Jennifer? I would still like to see if by a very large chance there is a fingerprint on it that would help in solving the crime. I realize it is a preposterous idea, but I have to try. Nowadays, there are more advanced tests."

Freddie looked hopeful, and Jennifer was relieved to see him in this hopeful state. "Of course you may. I am so glad I found the clock, Freddie. I do hope with all my heart there is something out there that will help you resolve any small portion of the past and give you peace."

20

Rick and Ring were jogging through the snow, hoping to see something unusual. He wanted to find a reason to end his suspicion of Latino Pizza. *These guys are careful and smart. They covered everything, and even Ring was fooled.* Tonight, however, something was in the air. Ring had his tail up higher than usual, and he was running as though the streets were bare, not slippery with ice.

Approaching a corner, Rick saw the van that belonged to the bakery. He made a note to himself to ask Jennifer how long the bakery stayed open. However, Gabe, the store owner, probably used his van for himself, as well as the business. *The guy has to get home somehow.* He saw the van from the front, and when it turned he saw the side. Just as the van turned again, Rick grabbed Ring by the leash and quickly hid in the bushes. Gabe was driving, but he had not spotted him yet. What Rick saw was highly unusual. Gabe was driving the bakery van, but it had the Latino Pizza magnetic sign on one side.

It was getting dark but still not too dark to see the difference. Luckily, there was a streetlight where Rick was hiding, and sure enough one side said one thing and the other said another "Latino Pizza." Quite possibly the other Latino Pizza sign had fallen off. *But why a pizza sign on a bakery truck?* Rick decided to take a picture of it with his phone and hoped that Gabe would not see the small flash.

Ring was quiet but tugging at his leash. He wanted to see more, but the van scooted out of his vision and was gone. If Rick had his car, he would be quietly following him to see where he was going. However, he could backtrack and see if he could find the sign on the road. Ring looked as though he was up for it, so maybe it was a good idea. His shift was over at seven in the winter months; this gave him one last official business before he set off for home. It was on his way, which made it an even better idea.

Outside some Christmas house lights were still on, and the streetlights were also giving off enough light to see. They appeared haunted with strings of icy cobwebs strung to their tops. Ring was running now, and both were breathing hard. The air was full of ice crystals, and then Ring stopped very suddenly. There lying in the bank of snow half over a ridge was the sign Rick was looking for. He picked it up gingerly, wearing his woolen gloves. The underside was glassy with ice, and this may have been why it slid off the bakery van. *What to do with it now?* Rick decided to take it downtown to the station in the morning, but for now he had a long walk home.

As the two walked home, the best they could with the sign between them, Rick was thinking of Freddie. He had to see him soon. In the winter months with Freddie being at the shelter, he was not employed by Rick and he was sorely missed. He enjoyed the camaraderie he had created with Freddie.

The next day at the bakery, the first thing Rick did was surreptitiously check the van. There was no evidence of any other Latino Pizza sign on the van, and for a short breath of time Rick thought he was mistaken.

Jennifer was at the bakery looking like sunshine today, and Rick just watched her pour coffee and chat with the customers. She looked happy, and he was sure something special had happened the night before.

"Jen, hey, Jen."

Jennifer turned and stared at Rick. *What is it lately that everyone is calling me Jen?* "Hey, Rick, what's up?"

"Do you still get off at three?"

"Yup, still do."

Rick looked around for the manager, but he was not in plain sight. When Rick told Jennifer he would stop by at that time and walk her home with Ring, she didn't think it was a big deal. She thought for sure he was intrigued by Freddie and his sleeping disorder at her Christmas dinner.

When 3 o'clock arrived, Rick made a cursory look around the side of the building and the van was gone. Jennifer was waiting for him outside by the lonely picnic table embedded in snow. She was sitting on the bench looking quite chilly, so he and Ring stepped up their pace.

"Jennifer, Jennifer!" Rick yelled into the cold air.

Jennifer rose and joined him, walking in the direction of her condo.

"What's up, Rick? You sound as though something very exciting has happened." "Actually, it has. Can you tell me anything different about Gabe lately?"

"No, why?" Jennifer rewrapped her plush woolen scarf around her neck and sped up her own walking pace.

"Just curious. We at the station are keeping a watchful eye on all the white vans in town; it looks as though there is some transporting of goods going on, but we have not been able to prove anything yet." Rick was reluctant to say any more, so he stopped.

"What kinds of goods, Rick?" Jennifer was now curious.

"We are not sure yet, but some of the businesses may be moving goods together. Let me know if you see anything strange at the bakery, with Gabe or the van. No one is under suspicion, but we are making sure we have all of the details before we act on anything."

"No problem. Now do I have a story for you. Are you ready?"

"Yeah, sure, I am all ears, so to speak."

Jennifer laughed and looked at Rick with his earmuffs on. "So no earmuffs for Ring?" When Ring heard this, he jumped up onto her leg. Jennifer gave him a quarter of her afternoon snack she was harboring in her pocket.

"It is all about Freddie. My goodness, I had no idea."

It took the rest of the walk home for Jennifer to relate all she had learned about Freddie in the last few days. She talked of him with utmost respect and related the facts to Rick much like Freddie did to her. Just like Freddie, this helped her to deflect any emotion, so she was able to get through the toughest parts and not lose her resolve.

When she was coming to the end, she heard Rick say, "No kidding, no kidding."

"So, did you know any of this, Rick?"

Quietly, Rick confessed he knew nothing of Freddie's past, and he was a little stunned as they took the last few steps toward Jennifer's condo up and over the incline.

When Jennifer looked at him in the bright sunshine of the cold winter day, she saw tears in his eyes. "He actually had a wife and a daughter?"

Still in disbelief, he sauntered down the hill after giving Jennifer a huge hug. Ring, sensing his sadness, walked slowly to his right with his tail hanging down.

The next working day, Rick took the sign to the station. He had thought about Freddie all night and was still extremely sad. Freddie had done so much for him, and he had not even thought to ask him about his past. When Rick told his wife about Freddie, she was as surprised and as sad as he was. She had met him last Christmas when he was helping the Salvation Army sell trees.

Officer Cliff was just finishing up at his desk when Rick walked in with the Latino Pizza sign. "Looking for a free lunch?" Officer Cliff laughed and clearly advertising for others to buy as well...nice touch. Officer Cliff was still laughing as he pulled out the steel cabinet drawer and filed his last case.

"No, I am quite sure I will not be buying anything from these guys." Rick reiterated what had taken place the night before, and Officer Cliff listened intently. "There is definitely something going on."

"We need to put more men on this, sooner than later." Officer Cliff had foresight into where this might be heading and wanted to be prepared. He asked Officer Karen and Officer Blake to come into his office, and a meeting was set up for the next morning regarding a proactive approach to sniffing these guys out.

After Rick gave more details about the pizza sign on the bakery truck, the other officers agreed it was indeed strange and very unusual. Officer Cliff mentioned he would look into getting the sign fingerprinted because, as he told the others, Rick had good instinct and he felt as though fingerprint identity was a good idea. It would take a couple of weeks; things like this not directly related to a crime were low on the totem pole.

It was the end of January, and it appeared as though all of the questions in his head were solved. Rick had no worries about the sign, Jennifer, or Freddie anymore. He felt as though he could do nothing about the sign until fingerprinting came back. Freddie had a sorrowful history, but he still breathed a positive spirit into life and at the same time became an uplifting mentor to others. He knew Jennifer was seeing Carlos when she could. However, Rick had not seen Carlos for a while now and was determined to ask about him shortly.

Meanwhile, his wife was receiving increments as she took more courses and life was good. His grown kids were happily married, and he was now a very young grandfather. His former demons had abated and left him alone for good. Ring was now eating a huge meal and drinking like he was in the Gobi Desert when a call came in for Rick.

He had no idea who was calling as he approached the small space he used for an office and quickly picked up the phone. There was no answer on the other end, just a click.

"Who picked up the phone?" He walked all around the station to get an answer. Rick wanted to know how the person knew his name to ask for him.

Officer Karen mentioned she had picked up the phone, and the caller asked for him with his full name. He asked for Rick Csapo.

"So was it a male caller?" Rick wanted to clarify.

"Yes," Officer Karen confirmed. "However, he would not give up any identity or divulge in what he was needing to talk to you about."

"Thanks." Rick went back to his desk and sat down. Maybe there was a way to check the number.

He called the phone company, and as long as it was within a half-hour they could retrieve the number; the operator found it for him. It was the number of Latino Pizza. Now he was perplexed, now he wondered. *Had anyone seen me walking with the sign last night? Why would someone phone me and then hang up?*

"Did anyone phone for a pizza lately?"

Nobody remarked. He just saw a bunch of heads shaking no.

Anyway, why would they ask for me by my full name if someone else ordered a pizza?

At the meeting the next morning, Rick exemplified his concern after the haunting phone call. Officer Cliff mentioned he did not want Rick going near the business again. They were identifying him with his dog on the street, and he had undoubtedly been spotted there many times. It was agreed that Freddie would do the undercover work and be given ears so he could phone when he saw something out of the usual, like the bakery truck backing in and loading or unloading anything suspicious.

"What do you think they are doing?"

Officers Rick, Karen, and Blake were hearing for the first time the chance that both companies were in on a scheme.

"We are looking out for Carlos and Fernando. These are two innocent young people whom we know of so far. We do not want them to be caught up in the middle of a drug war. This is what is happening according to the downtown station in Vancouver. Drugs are being sliced through the interior somehow and taken by truck to the coast for distribution. We are not clear as to who the perps are as yet, but we will soon. So far, with Rick finding the sign on another truck, it may look as though both trucks from both the bakery and pizza outlets are being used to transport. It is also interesting that absolutely no one heard of Latino Pizza before a few weeks ago, when it opened up. I have to admit their pizza is good. My wife ordered it for the kids not too long ago, and it was the best pizza I have ever tasted." Officer Cliff stopped talking.

Other questions flew by Officer Cliff, and he handled them diplomatically and with assurance that they were doing all they could for now until other facts proved themselves. They were waiting for the sign to come back, although even if Gabe's fingerprints were on it, it would not help right now. Of course, his prints would be on it if he mounted the sign, but his fingerprints would be on file only if he was involved in the law. Officer Cliff had foresight on this as well. Like a good cop, he had a hunch that this guy was on the cutting edge of something dark. When Rick heard this, he could not wait to warn Jennifer and Freddie of the possible danger. He might even get Jennifer to take a couple of days off when the time was right. He also knew Gretchen worked there and others, but the time would come when they might have to go in for this guy who had a reputation of intrigue and temperament. Jennifer would certainly contest to that.

He, however, would not want her to know right away; it would make her jumpy and inefficient. The less she knew, the better.

The chance came sooner than Rick thought. Gabe was bringing in a freezer from another source one weekend, and when Jennifer went to work the next day she saw a huge space cleaned out in the back room and a very large older white freezer inserted into its place. There was no way she could tell what was in it or what it was for; it was locked.

When Rick heard about this new development, he thought it was curious, but the fact that Gabe would not tell any of his employees what it was for became a suspicion.

A couple of weeks after that, Jennifer wanted to know if she could use it for her next shipment of Belgian chocolate. Gabe almost had a heart attack right in front of her. He threatened that if she tried to use it she might want to consider another job location.

"Ouch," Rick yelped when Jennifer said this.

When he indicated this to Officer Cliff, he put other detectives on instance alert and now it was a waiting game. A game when other facts of evidence came to light and there would be a reason to go in there. The first time the station had a pull toward sinister since the murder of Carlos' sister. They were not yet aware of the murders of Freddie's family. This was not revealed to the station house as yet; only Jennifer and Rick knew of this so far. They were waiting before they divulged this case to others.

Freddie needed time to get over his recent confession, and once he felt comfortable he agreed he would come into the station and tell Officer Cliff what had changed his life that many years ago. There was so little chance that relaying his past would bring the killer to justice so Freddie fell silent.

Meanwhile, he had taken the clock from Jennifer's mantel and found a very expensive but top fingerprinting analyst in a larger city. Freddie was not going to reveal which city, as he wanted complete privacy until something showed up, either a fingerprint or a hidden key.

21

Officer Cliff was going crazy. His office and stationhouse were far busier than he had ever anticipated. Ever since Rick and Ring came back with more data and more information, there was total mayhem.

Rick and Ring were on the street the day Jennifer went missing from her shifts. The staff at the bakery covered her shifts but still no word from Jennifer. Gretchen was beside herself. She knew that Jennifer had never missed a day and therefore something was dreadfully wrong. Rick was the one to find out what happened. He was asked to check her condo and then the hospital. Jennifer was not at her condo, but she was at the hospital. Rick found her room, and then he heard her story.

"I was afraid to call someone. He was so angry, and then when he would not let me into the freezer to let me freeze my shipment of Belgian chocolate that came in late that morning, I did not know what to do. Of course, when I mentioned what was the big deal, he lost it."

"Who are you talking about?" Rick was adamant.

"I am talking about Gabe; he has been very difficult lately. I do not know what is in that freezer that he is protecting, but it sure is not for the use of the bakery or the staff." Jennifer adjusted the bandage on her head.

"So, Jennifer, what happened?"

"Well, I was direly disappointed, so I challenged him on it, of course—dumb me. In order to stop me from trying to lift the lid, he said it was locked. I could see the lock on it, but well, yes, due to the fact that I am a little stubborn, I looked for something to open the lock. Sure enough, I found an item that looked like a hairpin and I started to pick the lock. Can you believe that I tried to pick a lock? There is no way that I would do that in other circumstances, but I wanted my many boxes of chocolate to be in a freezer so they would stay fresh and able to be used for my many displays."

"Gabe should be appreciative of your decorating skills in the bakery and the fact that it has increased his business." Rick was supportive of her work.

"Well, I wish that were true, but it is not. Gabe saw me and became very angry; he took a look at what I was doing with the lock and immediately saw red. My grandmother would say seeing red was being in the temper zone, and trust me, he was definitely in the temper zone. He grabbed my arm, wrenched the item away that I was using to pick the lock, and then struck me on the side of the head. I fell and hit my head against the side of the freezer. Yikes, that was hard. At first, it was no big deal and then I felt dizzy. I quietly left through the back door and was very glad that my shift had just finished (it was 3:00), and in came Gretchen and the other girls, but they did not see me; they came in at the front."

Rick listened with serious concern. He knew he would be telling Officer Cliff about this and that there would be a visit to the bakery to see Gabe. This was in the workplace, definite assault with bodily harm, and now Rick was very interested in the contents of the freezer.

"What on earth could he be protecting that was so important?" Rick looked sideways at Jennifer as if she would have the answer.

"I have no idea, but one day we will all find out and I hope the little well, I cannot swear, has something in there that will send him to prison."

"So, Jennifer, when you are discharged you will be going straight home. Officer Cliff and the staff have had a meeting, and we have a couple of businesses under scrutiny so we are asking that you take some time off."

Jennifer did not have to be told twice; she was more than happy to stay away from a job where there was violence. "But what about Gretchen and the others on staff? They may also be in danger." Jennifer's voice was full of empathy.

"Not unless they want to see the contents of the freezer and try to pick the lock." Rick gave his signature grin.

"Oh, I see what you're saying, you think I was being a little insane?"

"Well, weren't you?" Rick grinned again.

"Okay, maybe, but he drives me crazy." Now it was Jen's turn to produce a small grin. "As long as Gretchen and the other girls are safe, I will definitely stay away until all of the issues are dealt with and things change."

"Good, but now I must go and follow up on some leads. Ring is tied up outside in front of the hospital, and sure enough there will be someone who complains that there is a canine in a medical venue." Rick rose to leave and, like the gentleman he was, took Jennifer's hand and then brushed the back of her hand with a slight kiss.

"Have you heard anything from Carlos?" She looked worried.

"Now Jennifer, I am a police officer, not one to keep tabs on boyfriends who are not available."

"Will you let Freddie know that I am here? Hopefully, he will be able to come and get me when I am discharged. He can drive my car. Here are the keys." Jennifer was reluctant to ask Rick to pick her up. He was a friend, but first and foremost he was an officer and she thought it would be inappropriate to ask.

"Yes, I will tell Freddie you are here; he will pick you up and take you home when you are ready." Rick left and, turning around, he smiled at her. Jennifer slept.

125

• • •

Freddie had received the results of the lab. He was absolutely elated with what he had found out. There were many fingerprints on the mantel clock. He knew three of the four that were listed. He knew one would be his own. One would also belong to Jennifer, and the other would belong to the antique store owner. The fact that there was one more made Freddie reel with excitement. Who could it be and, more importantly, how would he find out who it was? The lab said they would run more tests, meaning they would try to match it up with any police data in fingerprinting. The only thing Freddie had to do was produce his own fingerprints, the fingerprints of Jennifer, and the fingerprints of the store owner for a match. He had to find Jennifer and tell her his astounding news. He contemplated on the fourth pair of fingerprints or rather the sampling. It was found under the clock right next to the tab that opened to the inside. The lab mentioned the print was very old but still faint enough to make a match if they had one.

When Freddie rang the doorbell at Jennifer's condo, no one answered. Freddie knew she was off work, but it was already going on 4:00. Maybe she went shopping.

As Freddie was walking down her driveway, Rick pulled up onto the slushy asphalt and hollered, "Where have you been, partner? I have been looking all over for you."

"I have been looking for Jennifer. I came here first as I was in the area and her shift is over; she must be out shopping." Freddie stood in the slush.

"Jennifer is okay, but she is currently in the hospital with a bandage on her head."

As Rick unravelled the story, he had to hold Freddie back from running to the bakery and thumping Gabe in the head himself. "Here are the keys to her car. She will be discharged in about an hour. I checked when I left. She wants you to take these keys and drive her car to pick her up. Could you do that today, Freddie?"

"You bet, no worries." Freddie tried the keys in the car door before Rick left to make sure they were hers, and then he started the ignition. He was about to back out when Rick stopped him.

"Do not let Jennifer go near the bakery, even if she thinks she forgot something or feels the need to schedule shifts or see the girls. We are running a take down on Latino Pizza and the bakery as soon as we receive the final go-ahead from Vancouver. We know that Gretchen and the rest of that staff are exempt, so we are focussing on Gabe and Owen, the boss at Latino's. There is word that between these two there is a definite drug smuggling operation, and our city is being used as a gateway for a larger drug 'ring' in Vancouver."

As soon as Ring heard the word "ring," he was all over Rick and tried to jump up to see Freddie in the car as well. They both laughed, and Freddie threw him the remains of the hamburger he had kept in his pocket. *I have to get rid of this homeless habit of keeping food in my pocket.*

There was no way Freddie was going to let anything else happen to Jennifer. She deserved much better. He was going to look after her and set himself up in her spare bedroom if she was in agreement. There was no way he was going to let someone like Gabe—or anyone, for that matter—bully her or rip away her chances of having a safe and happy life.

When Freddie picked her up, she was happy to see him. It hurt him to see the bandage on her head. It hurt him even more to see the little bit of fear in her eyes, even though she tried to hide it. *I am not a violent man,* Freddie thought to himself, *but I would love to go and make a mess of that guy, the guy who hurt this beautiful young lady, like a surrogate daughter to me. Hopefully, Rick and the station will find a way to smoke him out and then we can rid the city of bad influences to protect the young here who just want to work hard and be safe.*

As Freddie drove Jennifer home, there was the shrieking and shrill of a police car spinning past them. They looked in the opposite lane to see Officer Cliff and Officer Karen with eyes focussed straight ahead. There was no sign of Rick and Ring. *They may be at the scene, already keeping an eye on Gabe so he does not suspect and bolt,* Freddie thought. Ring was good at trapping an assailant in a corner, and even though he was a kind and gentle dog he knew his job. If he was told to stay, his teeth would be showing, jaw gnarled, and the trapped person would have no chance to run. Ring could do his job for hours on end in one corner.

When Jennifer arrived at her condo, she had Freddie to serve her this time. It was a beautiful father-and-surrogate-daughter relationship. A few weeks ago, it was Jennifer helping Freddie through a tough time with the mantel clock and memories of his murdered wife and daughter. Now it was his turn to help Jennifer feel comfortable. He went to prepare her a hot drink. He knew she liked chocolate, and after searching her kitchen, just as he suspected, she had a little stash of Belgian chocolate in her cupboard. He melted the chocolate and added hot water and floated miniature marshmallows in it that he had also found in the cupboard. Jennifer was ecstatic. "How did you know?"

"How did I know? How could I not know that you love chocolate with all the chocolate you have in the bakery?" Freddie chuckled.

Jennifer felt warm and woozy, and then Freddie covered her up with the thick comforter and she abruptly fell asleep. There was no time to tell her about the fingerprints and what he had discovered at the lab. *Oh, well,* he thought, *that can wait.*

When Jennifer woke up, she was very hungry. She felt a little awkward that Freddie was walking her through all of the steps of healing and getting better. He had no idea what to cook for her, so he improvised. He took out some rice and read the package, took out some pork chops, heated a pan, laced it with cooking oil, and then decided to chop up some produce for a salad. While he was preparing the food for dinner, he asked her if she was all right to sit up and listen to his story about the mantel clock.

Jennifer was aghast as to what Freddie had to share regarding the fingerprints. Freddie wanted to go to the fingerprinting lab as soon as possible to record the match, as well as drive to Vernon and meet with the man who sold her the clock. Freddie also wanted to talk to the man and have him describe the seller of the clock. Even after ten years, Freddie was certain there had to be a way to find the man with the accent. Jennifer sat and listened without interrupting; she had always been a good listener.

After dinner, a full tummy and a few drinks of anisette Freddie implored upon Jennifer that she needed to go to bed. He found her meds and gave her the pill that the doctor had prescribed for her.

Before he covered her up, he asked if he could stay in the spare bedroom and be there to take care of her. She was immediately flattered and mentioned that it would be no problem for Freddie to stay. She indicated that she would sleep much better and feel more relaxed with someone in the house, especially at night.

Freddie watched her fall asleep. He cleaned up the kitchen and then found a good book to read. Jennifer had an incredible array of books to choose from on all three of her alphabetically organized bookshelves. He chose a book called *The Orphan Train* by Christina Backer Kline, one that he knew in some way he could relate to because he felt like he was an orphan himself trudging through life.

When Jennifer woke up, Freddie served her a delicious breakfast of eggs, bacon, toast, and a selection of fruit. Jennifer was so glad that Freddie had stayed. Her doctor had indicated that she was able to remove her bandage that morning only if she did not have a headache. Jennifer did not have a headache. She laughed because she acclaimed it to Freddie and the drinks he implored her to drink the night before—chocolate and anisette—what a great combination to feel totally relaxed, thus no headache. Freddie wanted to stay one more night to make sure Jennifer did not feel dizzy, did not feel compelled to go to the bakery, check on the girls, or make changes in the shift schedule. He indicated to her that everyone knew she was all right. Freddie stayed one more night.

· · ·

Nobody knew if Gabe could be dangerous, so Rick was at the bakery every hour and Gabe was beginning to suspect. Rick saw him on his phone texting someone. He was quite sure it was Owen at Latino's Pizza, warning him that something was coming down. It all came down at that moment. Five police cars came roaring into the parking lot of the bakery and Gabe heard them. He dropped his phone and ran out the back door. Rick had stationed Ring there, and there was no way that Gabe was getting past Ring. He showed his long pointed teeth and Gabe, the coward that he was, became stupefied with the dog in the corner—the corner where all of the trashcans lived. All of the police cars came to an abrupt stop. The customers in the store at the time were asked to quietly leave, that this was a potential crime scene. Once everyone had evacuated, the police found Rick outside handcuffing Gabe. Ring looked proud that he was able to detain him the way he did; his tail was up and his ears were like two antennae. Gabe had no idea what was happening; they had obviously caught him by surprise. There was no way he was going to be able to warn Owen. He resigned himself to the fact that yes, he was caught. The only thing that really bothered him was the look on the faces of his staff; Gretchen and the others looked disgusted but almost happy. They knew this was the man who hurt and terrorized their friend Jennifer. When the police took Gabe into custody, they literally did not care; they were elated that now Jennifer could come back to work and feel safe.

22

The United Airlines flight would be leaving soon for Bogota, Colombia, and Carlos wanted to be on it, but first he had to see Jennifer. The evening would come soon enough, but the first thing he had to do was climb the hill to find Jennifer and explain to her why he was going. There was a clip of cold air, and the snow was just starting to fall. He could tell that this February was going to be a grim one, and he was looking forward to a nice warm climate; he sure wished she was going with him.

There was so much to tell. He was trying to sort it out in his mind when he approached the final incline to her condo. He had to tell her about his aunt and uncle and how he found out about Fernando, who he now knew was his real twin brother. It would have been amazing enough to know he was a long-lost brother, but a twin made it even harder to believe.

When Carlos rang the doorbell, Jennifer answered with a sleepy look in her eye. *Her beautiful green eyes, so sexy, I would love to curl up and stay. I want to be with you, Jen, please tell me not to go.*

Jennifer took a step back and realized after rubbing her eyes that it was Carlos and immediately ran into his arms. "Where have you been? I have been thinking about you forever, and nobody else knew where you were, either." She flicked her hair up and fastened it so quickly, it was as though the pins were invisible. Her eyes became brighter, and she took him by the wrist and sat him down on the couch.

Carlos sat and just stared at her for the longest time. She stared back, and they kissed ever so softly. He kept his arm around her, and he nuzzled her ear. "Let's not talk right now. I just want to hold you."

"Is it serious? Something has happened." She could not take her eyes off his face, and there were worry lines on his forehead.

"No, nothing serious has happened. Something good has happened. I found my aunt and uncle. They were staying in Toronto with my aunt's sister and had not been home for a long time. That is why I could not reach them. They have permanently left their small apartment in Colombia and are coming to Canada to live. While in Toronto, they sent me a letter because they were afraid of the drug ring in Colombia that my father used to belong to when I was little. My father was killed because of the choices he had made there." Carlos looked away. He was embarrassed and did not want Jennifer to see how much this hurt him.

"Wow, did you tell them about Fernando and how he looks exactly like you?" Jennifer felt very excited that now they may receive answers.

"Yes, I did. It was very uplifting to know that he was my long-lost twin brother." Carlos smiled a great smile after this and almost jumped for joy. He was so happy to know that he now had a sibling. After losing his sister he felt lost, like he was drowning every week.

"Oh, my gosh, that is fantastic! Who would ever imagine that you would come to Canada and find a lost sibling! Oh, Carlos, I am so happy for you!" She leapt up and pulled him up as well and gave him a huge bear hug.

Carlos stood still and enjoyed this closeness. He wanted to wrap her up in the little blanket on the couch and carry her to the bedroom.

He knew there was a flight he needed to take that evening, but still he did not want to go.

"There is so much to learn about how Fernando came to be here. I talked to my aunt, and she told me part of the story but not the whole thing. Her other sister was my mother. Apparently, my mother had met a man before my father came along and she became pregnant. The man she had Fernando and myself with did not want both boys but said he could take only one; otherwise, he could not pay to keep her. He paid my mother money this whole time, but nobody knew this, even the man she eventually married, the one I thought was my real father. When my mother died and my aunt and uncle took me in, he continued to pay for me. I do not know who he is or where he lives even to this day. Fernando says he knows, but he is afraid to say too much because his adoptive parents have done so much for him and they know that his real father has many dealings with the law. He is a criminal, so Fernando will not speak of him."

Jennifer had quietly walked to the kitchen the whole time Carlos was talking because she could see that he was fading fast and she wanted to get him a drink. She knew that he liked Mexican beer, so she produced a bottle for him and he drank half as soon as his story ended. "What was the rest of the story your aunt did not tell you?" She was so struck by this story that she wanted to hear more.

"I do not know as yet. I will find out when I see her." Carlos almost cringed at this, as he did not want Jennifer to know he was going anywhere yet.

"You are going to see her?" Jennifer stopped the bottle she was drinking halfway to her lips.

"Yes, I will make a stop in Toronto on my way back."

"On your way back from where?" Jennifer stopped drinking.

"From Colombia."

"You are going to Colombia....When?"

"Tonight. My plane leaves early this evening. Flight 1007 from Kamloops to Houston to Bogota."

Jennifer said nothing. She rose from the couch and went over to the fridge, mindlessly looking as though there must be something in there that she desperately needed.

Carlos came up behind her and put his arms around her waist from behind. She melted into him and started crying. "At Christmas, we could not be together, now we still cannot be together. Why is this so hard?" She turned and looked at him and saw the yearning pain in his eyes.

"I will not be gone long. I need to finish some business in Bogota for my aunt and uncle and visit my mother's grave one last time. There is money in their bank account that they have given me authorization to take out, and this money will be a new start for them and for myself here in Canada. They have already paid for my first year of university, and so I have deep gratitude for them. I must do this." Carlos resigned his voice to a small whisper.

Jennifer looked at him. She was proud of whom he had become considering. Like her, he had to squelch down his non-existing parents and carry on. "Yes, you must go, but how long will you be?"

"Just long enough to complete the business and to pack up and ship the furniture my aunt and uncle left behind when they vanished one night."

"How do you know you will be safe there? What if there are drug lords looking for you? What if they find you in that same apartment?" Jennifer had numerous questions.

"It has been over three months since my aunt and uncle left. These people look once, maybe twice, and then look no more. They have no time, and they move on. If any neighbours see me, they think I am moving in or I am a hired mover to relinquish the furniture that has been there for weeks. Do not worry. I used to live there, and some of the neighbours who were our friends will look out for me and keep me safe." Carlos took a deep breath.

Jennifer did not want him to go; she wanted to keep him as long as she could, but the next question needed to be asked. "When do you have to leave?"

"In two hours, I must arrive at the airport to be there for an international flight. I want you to be with me, Jen. We will take your car. I will start shoveling the driveway now. The snow is still very light. We will have a great dinner, and then we will make love before we go to the airport."

Jennifer looked as though she was going to jump off a cliff. Her face masked such surprise, but at the same time it was mixed with excitement.

"Well, then, Mr. Colombia, let's get moving." Jennifer dipped down to retrieve a roasting pan from the drawer below the oven, took meat out, and started making dinner.

Carlos put on his coat, found a shovel in her tiny garage, and went outside to shovel. The dinner was hot and tasty, and they both felt warm on the inside from their meal, a couple of drinks, and then a beautiful time together.

When they arrived at the airport, Carlos sat holding Jennifer's hand until the ticket agent called his flight number, and then she kissed him hungrily and said her goodbyes. Jennifer waited for the plane to soar into the sky, and then she drove directly home. It was snowing heavier now, but the snow was landing so softly it looked like a beautiful Christmas card. She drove into the driveway, entered the house, and put her things down. Jennifer went into her bedroom curled up with her woolen blanket and cried herself to sleep.

When Jennifer woke up, it was much later in the evening. She felt numb and non-responsive but wondered why it felt so quiet. The stars were shining through her bedroom window, and she realized she had not closed the curtains. It was absolutely beautiful. The sky was as clear as black velvet, and the stars looked like diamonds randomly thrown upward. She stood watching this panoramic view from her bedroom window and felt lucky to have someone who cared so deeply for her. She could not stop thinking of Carlos, and then she saw a brilliant star, more brilliant than the stars around it, and wished on that star. She hoped and prayed for Carlos. She prayed he would come home safely to her and that there was nothing, absolutely nothing in Colombia that would hurt him. She prayed for an angelic ring around him and that any drug lord would not be in his vicinity and that he would be sheltered and safely snuggled away with his neighbours if there was any danger. She felt good about this and at peace. Finally, Jennifer brushed her teeth, changed into her pyjamas, found her way under the covers, and fell into a long, sound sleep.

• • •

Carlos arrived tired and dirty and then reluctantly retrieved his luggage at the airport. He took a cab to his old neighbourhood and wished he was not there. All he could think of was Jennifer. He dreamt of her on the plane and could not get her image or kisses off his mind. In the early dawn of morning, he could vaguely see the house where his aunt and uncle took him in and then his neighbour coming home from work. He dare not hail him down, as he did not want to bring any attention to himself. He had the key to his aunt and uncle's apartment and, after climbing three flights of stairs, walking around numerous bags of rubbish and garbage, he let himself in. There was a definite feeling of haste in the room. He could tell that his aunt and uncle left quickly. It looked as though they were demanded to leave. There were photo albums on the floor and pictures ripped out. There were utensils spilled from the kitchen drawer and papers strewn. Maybe someone had come after they left. Maybe they left just in time—he had no way of knowing. These questions he would not ask anyone nearby because he did not know if they were bribed to say nothing. All he knew was that the few items of furniture he might not even pack and ship. He felt as though he would just leave them to a poorer neighbour and get on the next flight home. He would go to the bank tomorrow to retrieve the funds he was given authority to withdraw; he would ask for bank drafts or better still have the funds transferred to his own account in Canada. Once this was done, he would then visit his mother's grave. He would buy flowers from the local vendor, for the last time have his favourite meal in Colombia, Ajiaco, a very popular soup, and then head home.

Carlos fell asleep on the couch and woke up with a start. The heat was unbearable. He had wished for a warmer climate, but this was insane. He had forgotten how the heat could make one feel. His head was spinning, and he realized his thirst could not be ignored. Going to the fridge proved pointless, as there was absolutely nothing in it and the smell was nauseous. Just then a humble knock came to the door, and Carlos stood frozen.

"It is Pedro from the apartment below. Carlos, are you there?"

"Yes, it is me." Carlos ran to the door and quickly unbolted the three locks he had fastened last night.

"Hola, I heard you were coming back. Your aunt and uncle told me from Toronto; they scribbled a little note. Are you all right?"

"Yes, Pedro, thank you. Are you yourself safe?"

"Yes, there was a problem not too long ago. They have left now. They are convinced your aunt and uncle will not return. Luckily, there was no trouble for the rest of us. We all kept our bolts on and stood very still, breathless as though they were not here."

"What happened? Why were they here?"

"We do not know, as we all stood very still and did not talk to anyone."

"Was it a gang or just street robbers?" Carlos wanted to know who it was that was terrorizing his family in Colombia.

"We heard there was still much money owed by someone from the past long ago. There was no more waiting." Pedro looked scared even saying this.

"You listened and heard well, thank you. I do not know who they were talking about, but I am glad you are all safe. Pedro, would you like some furniture? I will not be taking or shipping these items." Carlos stood back to let Pedro see what was left, and then he heard him gasp.

"Oh." He went in and ran his hand over the backs of the couch and the chairs. "These is real beautiful, real beautiful. I think it is what do they say, damask."

"Yes, it is fine furniture, Pedro. This a golden colour, and it is called damask. It has a little rise to the fabric, which gives it a textured look." Carlos stood close.

"Of course, I would love these. But why me, Carlos, why give this to me?"

"You have been a good friend, and you have looked after my family well."

Carlos could see the tears in the old man's eyes, so he quickly walked to the other furniture and pointed out all of the items he would be leaving behind in the care of Pedro. This was all his now.

Pedro walked humbly away and went immediately to bring four friends and relatives to help him carry it out. He worked so quickly, it was as though maybe Carlos would change his mind.

The next day, Carlos visited his mom's gravesite with flowers, kept his previously arranged appointment at the bank, had his favourite meal, and flew home that very same night.

23

Life in Colombia was hard. Gabe's life turned him into a villain and a thief. There was a time when he lived freely with his mom and many siblings, but once he became of age he was expected to help support the family like his older brothers. There were two choices, education or crime. Education was expensive, so Gabe was forced into crime. If it was not for the drug lords, he and his family would not have eaten or survived. Gabe's family knew their rules and their ways, but they still wanted out. Getting out was the hardest of all; his father wanted out also but he was killed, found later at the bottom of a lake.

When Gabe was told to follow a lead to Canada, he did not hesitate. He was still young and thought he had a chance. The drug lords were now pushing their lines through all of the ports, and the port of Vancouver was one of the busiest but it was so well maintained and so controlled, the risk was slighter.

There was also an additional factor. Many Europeans who arrived in Colombia—Bogota, especially—were talking. There was much discussion on the previous war, and wealth incurred. The wealth discussed had nothing to do with the drug ring. It had a brand-new look at how to acquire wealth. Gabe knew many cousins, as well as his sister-in-law, who listened carefully while working at the numerous high-class restaurants around the city. The Europeans were in a mindset to get their wealth back that was shipped to the States and Canada during World War II. Many pieces of art were shipped to keep them safe from the Nazis, and thus they remained hidden for years. They were hidden in many places where no one would think to look—old farmhouses, deep in the ground behind brick walls, and some hidden where only a key would reveal their secret.

Gabe listened to these stories and kept a document as to the details of what he heard. He interviewed all of the relatives he knew who worked in the venues where the Europeans talked. They were more than happy to feed the information to Gabe and his cohorts for a little extra cash.

Once Gabe heard the names of wealthy persons still existing, he was adamant to find them regardless of the cost. So he went to Canada, stationed himself there, and set up a business. This business would be the one that would be a front for his coerce activities.

It was during his documentation of the details that he discovered the secret keys that were planted. He had heard about this from one of his cousins quite a long time ago, but now more information had surfaced about how secrets were kept. Many Dutch people, especially those who were ardent watchmakers and clockmakers, had discovered an incredible way to hide keys. The older men of this culture were very astute and, for years unbeknown to others, had creatively hidden keys inside the clocks they had made—mantel clocks, to be exact. Of course, the only mantel clocks with the sacred keys in them belonged to the generations of Dutch clockmakers and then they were passed down to their families.

Today, it was very possible that the grandchildren of these clockmakers were the ones who controlled the destiny of the clocks. Gabe had to find out where they lived and who they were. He was able to do just that. He had a sister who was absolutely brilliant and able to research records back to the time of this incredible find. He used

Rosie and her expertise to locate any Dutch immigrants to Canada over the last sixty years, and she did just that. She found first, second, and third generations.

Once Gabe knew this, he put his plan into action. Out of all of the addresses and locations Rosie listed, there was one grandson who lived right here in the same city. He was the grandson of a brilliant watchmaker who lived in Amsterdam during the war. When Gabe heard of this, he found the house and stalked it. Numerous times he saw the car gone just after lunch. Nobody was ever home at that time, and one day he checked out his theory. He rang the doorbell and pretended he was a delivery man, but there was nobody home.

After three weeks of careful surveying, he concluded today would be the day to enter the house, steal the clock, and find the key, which would invariably bring him many riches. Breezing out of his car so he would not look too stern and official, he walked up to the front door. He made this look as though he had done it many times. With his credit card, he unlocked the door and prayed there was no alarm. If there was an alarm, he had a story all ready.

Once inside the foyer, he immediately spotted the clock on the mantel of the fireplace. He stole softly across the carpeted living area and, reaching for the mantel clock, he turned around to the sound of voices. He tiptoed back to the door and there they were, coming out of the kitchen, licking spoons as though they were both making cookies and licking the dough. He acted fast and pushed them back into the kitchen, and from that day on Freddie had no family. Gabe has had little sleep and lived with these demons for the past ten years. He wanted to kill himself the first day, but somehow he could not do that, so he drove to the next city and sold the clock—the evidence gone forever, so he thought.

From that day on, Gabe was not a man. He existed as though he did not belong anywhere. He floated through life as though a ghost and if he was found out to be a killer and/or a murderer he would gladly take the sentencing that would go with this. He saw too much in Colombia; he vowed he would never follow the steps and ways of the drug lords.

After years of living in Vancouver, Gabe thought it would be safe to come back to he interior and open a business. He met Owen in Vancouver, and when he learned the gateway city in the interior was a viable location for his business he chose it for his new life. Owen worked his pizza place, and between the two of them they were running drugs.

The idea came to them one night when they were at a loss as to how to secretly transport bags of drugs to Vancouver. The shipment came in on the train right through the desert city and were kept overnight in a container. Owen and Gabe had to drive their vans to the location and transport them off the train to be stored until other transport took them to the coast for distribution. Owen came up with the plan to load up his pizza boxes, and it was working so far. The boxes looked official, and when full they resembled a pizza that was to be delivered. The only catch was there were too many. Gabe had to store some at his bakery or the overflow would give them away.

Another problem that was arising was Owen realized that once his customers started to like the pizza he was making, people were arriving at his warehouse. He wanted the warehouse for other reasons, not for distribution of pizza. The risk was now too high. He tried to discourage in-store purchasing and set up only a delivery service. For the most part, it had worked well until this guy named Freddie and the street detective with his dog came sniffing around.

Then in came Carlos, who was so distraught after his sister was murdered that Owen was ready to pack up and find a new city. Of course, when Carlos asked him how he knew his sister in the pictures that Carlos had found in her house, Owen had nothing to say. He was waiting for that snoopy detective to come in and question him. He had all of the answers figured out in his head, but the days went by and his business became busier and busier, but the detective never did show up.

Little did he know that the whole department of police were going after Gabe and he was next. Once Gabe was caught they were going after Owen, but he did not know that yet. He was focussed on Fernando and Carlos and what the odds were that they would be related, not only related but twins. *How on earth did I get wrapped up with these guys from Colombia, plus where did they all come from—first Gabe, now these two? I must be crazy.* Owen was worried because he had killed the sister to Carlos. He was going with her, married to her, and even though there was a difference in age they had a nice relationship. All was going well until she became snoopy herself. She started to see the many pizza boxes filling up and realized how on earth could they be all pizzas. She lifted the lid of numerous freezers and saw the whole operation. The next day Owen went to pick up her up, and he was the only one who left the house. He threw her wallet out of her purse and made it look as though there was a robbery. He had not slept since.

Both Gabe and Owen knew it was just a matter of time for both of them. Between the bakery and Latino Pizza, there were too many people in this small town for secrets, so they had to act fast.

When Gabe arrived with the van that wintry night and had lost one of the signs, they knew their time was limited. They filled up the freezer in Gabe's bakery, and the next day their plan was to load it into their van and onto the next train container to be shipped out. There were many reasons they had to unload it in the city and then reload it. It had to be distributed in lots to off-guard the weight in each container. Each train container carried certain items, and the only way some were chosen for the drug trade were if they were lighter than others. So if a container held a large quantity of steel, it was quite likely at its capacity. However, if a container held grain, there was room for a different balance of weight. In the middle of the night, Gabe and Owen strapped the boxes to the undercarriage of the lighter containers.

They paid rail workers to let them know what container would handle the extra weight.

Once this was established, the operation went smoothly. All it took was watching and being careful, so the staff in either one of the businesses did not know what was going on. The freezer in Gabe's bakery was not plugged in, and the plug was hidden in case someone became suspicious. There was a little bit of ice slid down the side to keep the freezer in a good state. The ice was compacted as ice jackets in cloths, so the only thing that Gabe had to do was refreeze them overnight and get them back into place before any of his employees showed up in the morning. Otherwise, the cocaine-filled Latino Pizza boxes filled the freezer to the brim and it was locked.

Little did Gabe know that every day Rick appeared with his dog tied up outside, Gabe was being watched closely. The day Rick appeared off the street without the dog tied up outside was the day he became suspicious. He was lucky Jennifer was not there; it all seemed quieter without her and her crazy homeless friends. He was just starting to relax when he heard the sirens.

He looked out the corner of one window, bending as low as he could, and there were five police cars screeching to a stop at his front door. He scurried to the back and ran out the back door as fast as he could. The staff were moving fast to get out of his way. It did not matter because the wondering he had just before that about Rick's dog was now answered. There was Ring right there at the back door with a look that scared even Gabe. No sooner had Ring growled him into the back corner beside the garbage cans, but he positioned him so he was unable to run.

24

Carlos ran into the arms of Jennifer at the airport. He was never so glad to be home and to see her. He had visited his aunt and uncle in Toronto and promised them a new life in the interior of B.C. They could even live with him in his sister's house until they chose something on their own. His sister's house had three bedrooms, and he knew they would all be comfortable. When Carlos took Jennifer for lunch, she had much to tell. Little did Carlos know about the raid on Gabe and Owen. He was very happy to hear the part that Ring played in stopping Gabe from running out his own back door. Jennifer could see how that made Carlos smile all through lunch.

"He deserves whatever he gets." Carlos' body riveted when he heard what Gabe had done to Jennifer. He put his hand up to the side of her head to show his compassion.

"Well, it was probably worth being slapped and falling down, so we had more than one reason to swoop down on him. This way he will be charged on numerous accounts, assault, and drug trafficking to start." Jennifer felt happy to be sitting folded into the arms of Carlos while they ate their lunch on the same side of the bench.

"So, Rick and Freddie must be relieved that it is all over and no more snooping around in the garbage at the pizza place looking for clues. I must extend my appreciation to Freddie for helping you when you were discharged from the hospital. That guy is amazing. For a man who has lost his whole family ten years ago, he is amazing for the compassion he still holds for people. He is a true mentor and father figure, a true friend and companion." Carlos could not hold back the tears in his eyes for this man who helped his girlfriend through so much.

"Well, now for the best news." Jennifer could not wait to tell Carlos.

"You will not guess what I heard. It is not the best news because it is very painful for Freddie. Gabe has confessed to wiping out his family. Freddie was in the detective's office as an associate when Gabe was arrested. After three hours of interrogation, the police, trained in questioning, finally broke Gabe and he confessed not only to drug trafficking but the murder of Freddie's family. According to Rick and Officer Karen, who were also there, Freddie dropped to his knees and sobbed and sobbed incessantly. They helped him up and brought him immediately to my house, and I looked after him; he was very weak." One thing that Jennifer could not do at the time was tell Carlos who had killed his sister.

When Owen was brought in, the same team of police interrogators pummelled him with questions until he also confessed to not only drug trafficking but to the murder of Carlos' sister. She would wait until tomorrow to tell him this. Right now she wanted to revel in the warmth of his arms and feel his breath tickling her right ear.

• • •

When Freddie left to go to the shelter shortly after he brought Jennifer home from the hospital, he was asked to stay there until she and Carlos could pick him up. The staff at the shelter were more than gracious to check in on him in his room every twenty minutes or so. He was sleeping soundly, eating well, and then sitting up when Jennifer and Carlos arrived to retrieve him. He was going to be permanently set up in Jennifer's condo. Carlos would have his aunt and uncle, and Jennifer would have Freddie until they were married. Yes, Carlos had proposed and Jennifer had said an exuberant "Yes."

Once Freddie was picked up, he unloaded the few items he had and poured Jennifer and Carlos their favourite drink with Anisette. Of course, for Jennifer he brought out a little chocolate and marshmallows and she laughed.

"To the two people I care about deeply. Congratulations on your engagement, and may you both have a very special life together." Freddie had tears in his eyes once again, and after they all stood and clicked glasses. Freddie sat down. He could not help but look at Jennifer and say, "To the daughter I once had, but more importantly, to the daughter I now have."

Freddie was sobbing hard, and Jennifer went over and took the plaid handkerchief from his pocket and wiped his eyes. They all laughed and then they decided to order pizza, but this time it was not Latino Pizza.

At the bakery, much was being done. The business was up for sale, and until the end of the month the staff were allowed to continue to work and for this reason Gretchen was planning a huge party for Carlos and Jennifer. It was going to be a party of their dreams, and any customer who ever knew Jennifer was invited to attend.

Gretchen could not make it a surprise, as Jennifer was in and out of the bakery three or four times a day; she was quite the little manager. So even though Jennifer and Carlos knew the party was the day after tomorrow, they did not know the plans. Gretchen and her staff were drawing up the decorating of the bakery and the guest list on their lunch hour and then hid the papers so Jennifer could not see them.

"How many on the list so far?" Gretchen talked to all of the girls, and they agreed that including the staff and the customers that came in regularly and loved Jennifer so much, there were forty people. "Great, now we just have to figure out where to seat them all."

"I know, let's phone the rental shop and order some chairs and at the same time order some nice china. We all know how Jen loved to decorate the corners and how much she likes pretty things." The new girl was all over what Jen liked; she was quietly observant. Gretchen was on the phone and once she deposited the receiver Laura, the new girl gave her heads-up about her idea. At that she had Laura go directly to the rental shop and order what they needed. They all agreed on the decorations and colours, and the next night they would all come back to decorate.

It was a great feeling to be able to do something for Jennifer without Gabe in the background. Gretchen felt relaxed and content with the aspect of no boss looking over her shoulder. The only reminder of Gabe was that dreaded freezer in the back room. "I need to have Rick come and get this thing out of here," she gestured. "The sooner, the better."

The front bell chimed, and in walked the very person she was talking about at that moment. "Rick, hey, how's it going? By the way, congratulations on all of the arrests you and the station have recently made. Very impressive! By the way, is Ring outside?"

"Hey, Gretchen, how's it going? Lots of changes for you guys as well. Yes, Ring is outside. He is waiting for one of his favourite girls to pet him, and he looks a little hungry, don't you think?"

"I will get right on that." Gretchen was a quick study, and she rescued some biscuits and an old sandwich sitting on one of the tables not cleared yet and went out to nuzzle Ring and give him the treats.

When Rick was told about the freezer, he indicated it was the very thing he had come by to measure so he could phone a pick up company to deliver it to the station. He knew by the way Jennifer had talked about it there was something in there to discover. He knew it was going to further condemn Gabe in any court of law. He knew in his bones it was either a huge money drop or filled with drugs placed in plastic bags. *Wouldn't that be something if the little plastic bags were all lined up neatly in empty Latino Pizza boxes?* There was a report that some were slashed to the bottom of railcars and they actually were in Latino Pizza boxes. All of the officers were told to not talk to the press or reveal any knowledge of this until it was resolved and the blamed party was convicted.

Rick was true to his word, and within hours the freezer was picked up by a moving company. Rick had it deposited to the station shed, and with the help of one of the other officers they crow barred the lid open after cutting the chains.

True to what Rick believed, the freezer was full of Latino Pizza boxes and all of them filled with little plastic bags. He was not sure what the drug was until it was tested, but his guess would be cocaine. The amount of money this load would bring would be in the millions on the street.

• • •

"Wow, the colours are beautiful," was the first reaction from Jennifer after she erected herself from the crouched surprise shouts of her many guests. Jennifer never felt so warm inside, and the gifts kept flooding into the circle of friends where she was sitting. "Thankyou" was all she could say, over and over again.

Just then the door opened, and in walked one of the most handsome men all of the girls had ever seen. He quietly put his hat down on the counter and surveyed the crowd for the one person he came to see. It was Gretchen.

Gretchen was just bringing out a tray of hot rolls, and she almost dropped them. Right there in front of her stood Dustin, the handsome cowboy from the antique store in Vernon. "Howdy, ma'am. I sure hope I am not disturbing something of extreme importance," he drawled.

"You are definitely not disturbing anyone." Gretchen sighed. "Just sit your cute little butt down and I will get you some coffee."

Jennifer was giggling already. As soon as she could get Gretchen alone in the kitchen, she dragged on her arm and jolted her to the corner. "When did all this happen?"

"All what?" Gretchen slowly smiled and unwrapped Jen's fingers from her sleeve. "You know what I am talking about, you little brat, and you never told me?"

"Told you what?" Gretchen was going to stretch this out as long as the party would allow her.

"Why would he come today of all days? Why, Gretch?"

"Oh, okay, we have been talking on the phone. He retrieved the number of the bakery from the phonebook, and one day he just phoned up. He could not get me right away, as there was another shift, but he left a message and we have been talking ever since. He does look hunky, doesn't he?"

"Hey, you guys, we need more coffee and those delicious doughnuts!" Freddie took on the job of host when the girls had slid away.

Out in the bakery area, Carlos was keeping Dustin entertained and they were both laughing. Rick had entered their circle, and then they all stepped out into the sunshine to be with Ring.

Spring was fast upon them, and this was one rare day of sunshine. The snow was melted in the beautiful valley but sparkled white on the rolling hills. Some of the numerous trees in the downtown area were starting to bud pink, and white and brightness shone everywhere. The ubiquitous Ponderosa pine stood erect and proud, green in contrast.

The crowd of friends and customers surrounded Jennifer and Carlos, wishing them well. Over in the chocolate corner, Jen could see Dustin with his arm around Gretchen and they both looked so happy.

"So Rick, when is the trial for these guys that we brought in?" Freddie was all ears, and Carlos was coming forward into the tightly knit group to hear more.

When Carlos found out who murdered his sister, he went away for a couple of days to grieve. He felt sad that he treated her with such impatience, but now he felt better and was able to talk about it.

"So when do we know the outcome?" Carlos wanted this man put away as quickly as possible.

"We will be waiting for a long time to hear the outcome. These guys put our city in peril, and they will be sentenced accordingly. I am so glad they are not distributing drugs to the kids on the street. The fact that they were also murderers right in our own backyard makes my skin crawl." Rick looked around while he talked. He realized talking business in a public place was not professional, so he stopped.

"So, in the next few weeks we will know if Gabe had found a key in the mantel clock. According to the officers who questioned him, he was only able to tell about the crimes he committed so far and other details had to wait. Gabe had suddenly gone cold on them and was not talking. He went dead inside, and there was a situation in his cell. They had to take everything out so he would be safer. He went a little bit crazy." Rick had taken Carlos and Freddie to the far corner of the building and informed them so they would be at peace about it until other information was reported.

"Hey, you guys, get over here; we are cutting the engagement cake." Gretchen strode over with her arm around Dustin.

Carlos came over and planted a kiss on Jennifer's cheek. Freddie stood beside everyone, feeling like he now had a family. Carlos' aunt and uncle had arrived the night before and were there to support Carlos. Fernando was there with his adoptive parents. Rick's wife had also arrived, and there were more than forty customers who arrived to celebrate the engagement.

With little glasses, everyone toasted the newly engaged couple, and then everyone clapped when Carlos gave Jennifer a deep dip and pretended he was kissing her like they were already married.